THE INFINITY CIRCLE

∞

ALEX NICHOLS

THE INFINITY CIRCLE

ISBN: 978-1-7357035-0-3 - Paperback
ISBN: 978-1-7357035-1-0 - eBook

Cover Art and Design by Damonza

for darling lily

PROLOGUE

THEY SAY THAT anyone who isn't telling you the truth is trying to sell you something. I would know. I am an actor. My professional life has involved trying to present the imaginary as real. When I do my job well, people believe what they were seeing. Sometimes I believe it, too.

Perhaps you've seen me. For fifteen years I played Mira Thornton on *Wild Hearts.* Remember that daytime soap set at a winery in Northern California, the one with the kooky plot about the secret son who was locked in the attic? I played the family nanny, an ingénue in rag curls and swing dresses who wore a gold charm bracelet and pined for a troubled vineyard worker. I was told at my audition that Mira must have an *accessible beauty*, which is a veiled way of saying that I needed to be pretty but not beautiful. There are two types of beauty, you see: the type a woman aspires to and the type she envies because she can never attain. I was the former. It meant that the female viewers would relate to me, not wish me dead.

To this day, people come up to me at coffee shops and on the subway, telling me that they scheduled their college classes so they could watch the saga of Mira and Jacoby unfold. There is one episode they have never forgotten and mention with a tedious predictability. The fans call it "The Arabian Escape." (Soap episodes themselves never had titles. They were given sequential numbers in the order of which the episodes were taped. When you produce two hundred sixty new episodes a year, the imagination is spent.) My character was set to marry the playboy son of the central family, but her heart belonged to Jacoby, the earnest but emotionally damaged vineyard worker. As Mira stood outside the church, shivering alone in her white lace dress (she was an orphan, of course, and was to walk herself down the aisle) Jacoby rode up on an Arabian steed and pulled Mira up on it with him. They galloped off to a nearby hill town where they made love in a wine cellar.

We made the unlikely seem plausible. If legions of fans could believe that a man would jump on a horse and kidnap his love moments before she was to marry someone else, if they could buy that this was pure and in no way pathological, then we had been successful.

I believed it, too. That is where the trouble began.

CHAPTER ONE
NOW

The summer I turned forty-three, my husband Peter and I took a two-week trip to Italy. It was August, and beastly, but soon we were gorged on Titian, on burnt sienna skylines, on paper-thin pizza and carafes of red wine, and had all but forgotten about the heat. We had come to Italy to salvage our marriage, but the aesthetic pleasures had acted more as a cocktail than an elixir. Walking home at night, our bellies full, I looked around at the terra-cotta roofs and huge hanging moon and had to remind myself that I wasn't on a movie set. The surroundings could transport us but they couldn't transform us.

For our last few days we took a train through the Tuscan countryside to a medieval hill town. When we arrived, we pulled our suitcases past tour buses through the central square to our destination. I had booked us a hotel room with a balcony overlooking the cathedral piazza. There were pigeons resting in the bell tower's shade and hordes of tourists sitting on the lip of a fountain. Children splashed and shouted in its waters. An old man dipped his weathered hand into the trough, his dog snapping at the surface.

Peter collapsed on the bed when we got to the room, closing the blinds and switching on a tennis match. I went out on the terrace to take in the view. From inside the room, I could hear the sounds of a tennis ball hitting clay, the grunts of the players, the polite claps from the audience.

An umpire made a call. I thought of a t-shirt I had once seen: *in tennis, love means nothing.* In tennis and other things, I thought now. My mouth crinkled into a smile. I fished into my bag for my phone. There were three texts from my best friend.

page one: *are you coming up again this year? can't wait*
page one: *oh, I just saw instagram. I forgot you and peter are in Italy. lovebirds!!*
page one: *let's talk when you get home. k???*

Page was my oldest friend, my roommate at Barnard when I first moved to the city. We had a long-standing tradition of a late summer girls' weekend at her house in Katonah, much of it spent drinking cocktails by her pool while Page told colorful stories about her love life. I had accepted long ago that I was the boring half of the friendship. This would be the first year I would have news that might top anything she had to say.

I clicked on Instagram and scrolled through my feed. I had posted half a dozen shots from our trip, broadcasting to my 2112 followers images of gelato, canals, a fluffy orange cat sleeping on a scooter seat. There was only one photo of Peter and me, sitting across from each other at an outdoor table with enormous bowls of pasta in front of us. We were a study in contrasts: me with my thin salon blonde hair and fair skin that burned easily, Peter with dark wavy hair and a farmer's tan. The Spanish Steps were in the background. It had inspired hundreds of likes and six comments:

mattressfever: *aww, you two are so sweet!*
glitterbomb: *awesomeness!*
pageone: *jealous!*
mrswilson: *Hayes and I were there last year. Enjoy!*
JaneSays: *True love!*
ryano: *I'm a fan from your soap days. Where's Jacoby?*

The usual social media blather.

When we returned to New York in a few days, I planned to tell Peter that I wanted him to move out. We had been married eighteen years. In that time I had turned away from what felt now like an inescapable reality:

we were just existing together, not living. This had been true for years, since our son was small. But it had taken me years to face it.

One telltale sign of marital breakdown is when you can name a period of time since you have last had sex with your husband. I could go one better: I couldn't remember the last time we did. I could say with some certainty that we had done it at least once within this calendar year. It was probably one of those middle-of-the-night fumbles aiming for the lowest possible probability that we might be overheard. In terms of actual visceral memory of the experience, though, I was at a loss.

"I'm going out for a bit," I said, slipping my bag over my shoulder as I came in from the terrace. It held the room key, my phone, and a paper map of the town.

"Bring back some bubbles," he said, rolling over on his side lazily. That was one thing Peter and I had in common: a shared love of a nightly cocktail. In New York, it was more often a Grey Goose tonic or a vodka gimlet, but on this trip we had discovered a light prosecco we both liked.

As I left our hotel, the cathedral square was still jumping with activity. I moved away from it and climbed a steep cobblestone incline. There were clothing boutiques, cheese shops, a store that sold only herbs and olive oil. I kept walking in search of a view, ignoring my heart as it beat harder. I was wearing thin strappy sandals that were ill suited for stone walkways.

At the top of the hill, I found shade beneath a Gothic archway. I sat for a few minutes watching the human traffic go by. There was a group of curly-haired teenage boys laughing and slapping at each other, shouting out in a staccato language that echoed off the walls. An old man, stooped at the back, walked with a wooden stick.

A young woman in a yellow dress appeared. She was holding the hand of a chubby toddler. Something about that age, with the dimpled fists and the unsteady gait, always made me ache for Riley. He was now a wiry 18-year-old who would start his first semester at NYU in a few weeks. Peter and I had spent the weekend before our trip helping him move into his first apartment on Thompson Street. We had relinquished our Balinese day bed, a pile of linen, and two wine jug lamps to help him settle in.

A mother and child walked down the incline and out of my view. I closed my eyes, saying a private blessing for my son. It was noon in New

York right now. He was probably loping down the street, linking hands with Veronica, his new girlfriend. I pictured them stopping into a bodega to escape the heat, dipping into an ice chest to pull out two lime popsicles.

In my shoulder bag, my phone buzzed. I was hoping it was Cora, my agent, calling to give me more information on an audition she had set up for me the next week. It was a supporting role in a play and I was nervous and excited about getting back on stage.

"Mags, hi. It's Julian Barker." Her deep voice, dripping a Bronx dialect, was curiously intimate. She was immediately familiar although I hadn't talked to her in nearly five years. "I'm sorry to bother you."

"Julian, it's been a while. How are you?"

"I'm sorry to say I'm not calling for idle chit chat. I have some news. Are you sitting down?" This was Julian: brusque to the point of rudeness. She was a woman completely without artifice.

I told her that I was. My heart was beating fast as I took in her next words: "Hon, I'm sorry to tell you that Ian is dead. He took his own life."

Falling down a rabbit hole, I was now in Brooklyn in a red swing dress, my hair in rag curls. I was shutting the clasp on my charm bracelet as the cameras moved into place. Ian was standing in his blocking, gazing at me intently with his intense brown eyes. He was muttering something under his breath, reviewing his lines.

"God, what." It was all my mouth could allow.

"I know, hon. I was quite shocked when I heard the news. And now I'm contacting all of you in case this makes the news. I don't know that it will, of course. But I thought you might like to know."

"Thank you," I said, still at a loss for words.

"We're going to do a memorial here in the city next week at the Chapel of the Lamb here on Barrow Street. Do you know it?"

I didn't but I indicated that I would be there. I made a note of the day and time.

After a few more remarks, Julian and I hung up. I was alone now, sweating in the shade of the Gothic archway, allowing the news to sink in.

Ian Dorrit was my co-star for many years. He was my first real lover and my first experience of heartbreak. When he ended things – callously, abruptly – I got married and pregnant to forget about him. It didn't work.

And now he was dead.

❧

Our plane was late leaving Fiumicino so we arrived to JFK in the middle of the night. The airport was a strange ghost town in the hours between the last and first flights. Peter and I moved silently through immigration and customs, then picked up our bags and departed through the sliding doors. It was sweltering, even at 2 AM, and as we took a taxi back to our apartment, I could smell the jet fuel and gasoline still in the air.

The night doorman came out to help us with our bags. His name was Edgar and he had been on the job for a few years. The only things I knew about him were that he lived in the Bronx and had twin sons, a fact he mentioned more often at moments when tips were more likely.

I couldn't sleep so I spent the rest of the night doing laundry. We had a washer and dryer in the maid's room off the kitchen. I robotically pulled out summer cottons and soiled under garments, sorting them into heaps and watching as they spun in suds. When he was a baby, Riley had loved this room. I would find him pulled up onto his wobbly legs, his dimpled hands on the glass circle, mesmerized by the sounds of washing clothes.

As the sun came up, I walked to a bakery on Lexington. I browsed around for a bit, chatting to the baker about my trip, before I bought a fresh loaf of black bread and a chocolate chip muffin. I paid in cash, and walked the block and a half back to the apartment. There were few hints of the later oppressive heat that would shut us all indoors.

I found the doorman behind his desk, reading a freshly delivered copy of *The Daily News*. I handed him a paper bag with the chocolate chip muffin. He smiled warmly. It was my custom to bring him gifts from time to time, which he always received appreciatively.

"A woman died," he told me as he ripped into the bag. "She was trying to carry her stroller down the steps to the subway and she fell. They found her dead at the bottom, the kid still strapped in."

Edgar and I often commiserated like this; the cruelty of bad luck in contrast to our own good fortune. It was something we had in common.

The apartment was still quiet when I entered. In the kitchen I went about the daily ritual of breakfast. I mashed avocado, lime, chili flakes, and sea salt together into a paste. I served myself a thick slice of avocado toast with a mug of black coffee while Peter took a steam shower and left for the office.

Alone in the apartment, I turned on my computer and waited for it to come to life. I couldn't bring myself to Google Ian's name just yet so I thoughtlessly scanned through the morning headlines, the weather report, and some rug patterns my decorator had sent me. I was thinking of re-doing our living room.

After a while, I typed a name into Google. *Esther Oden.* There were a few generic entries, sites that wanted to draw me in by claiming to have information on her, but none of the standard social media platforms. I wasn't surprised that she kept a low profile.

I thought back to the day I had encountered her for the first time. As a favor to Barnard, my duty as an alum to network with undergrads that aspired to my field, I would sometimes talk to students who dreamed of TV work. We met at a café called Absinthe in the village. The interior was like stepping into Paris with its wicker chairs, movie posters, and a menu that featured citron presse, croque madame, and salad nicoise. When I arrived a bit early, she was already there, sipping an Orangina through a straw. She was nineteen and fat, with a straight bob that made her look like an overgrown child and the fashion sense of someone who wears whatever fits. I took an instant dislike to her on aesthetic grounds.

Over lunch we talked about Barnard, theater, her childhood in upstate New York. Her grandmother was a librarian in a small town. Esther dreamed of writing plays like her idol, Wendy Wasserstein. She loved *Wild Hearts.* She told me she had boxed up her grandmother's old VCR and brought it with her to Manhattan so that she wouldn't miss an episode.

She was enraptured when I told her about the set, about the cast, and especially when I talked about Ian. By the time the waitress had brought over the check, I felt a pang of guilt about my earlier mean-spiritedness. Show biz turned everyone into a potential competitor. My days of trying to break into the industry had made me instantly suspicious of wannabes. In an effort at kindness, I let her in on a secret: we had just taped the episode where Jacoby and Mira made love for the first time. Her mouth dropped open in excitement and awe. In a moment of experimental generosity, I gave her the name of the coordinator of our summer internship program.

"Veruca St. Clair," she said, writing it down on her palm. I took the ballpoint pen from her and wrote a tip on the credit card receipt and then signed my name.

We walked out into the fresh spring air on Bleeker Street. "See you on the set!" she called out to me as I walked away. Her overconfidence rankled me. I hoped I would never see her face again. But I had, when she turned up a few months later to do an internship with Julian and Veruca. That was nineteen years ago.

I typed Esther's name again and the name Burr, NY. I could still hear her voice in my head saying, "I'm from a town called Burr, as in Aaron, the guy who killed Alexander Hamilton." It was funny how the mind never forgets certain random details. This pulled up more information, including recent addresses in Ithaca, NY. I jotted them down and Googled my route. I had just enough time to get to Ithaca, do what I needed to do, and be at Page's by sundown.

I picked up my phone and texted Page. *If you can have a frozen margarita ready for me at 8, I'll bring dinner. xxoo*

Jetlag be damned, I was ready to spend some time with a friend and forget about the last twenty-four hours.

Or so I hoped.

CHAPTER TWO
THEN

I was lucky, I suppose. Growing up in western Massachusetts, I had watched soap operas here and there – on torpid summer afternoons, on housebound snow days – and dreamed of being an actress. There was something about it that pulled to me like no other aspiration. I dreamed of living a hundred lifetimes other than my own.

My mother was from a nearby Berkshire hill town, the oldest of six kids. When she was eighteen, her father packed up his red pickup and drove her down into the Pioneer Valley and helped her move into a boxy modern dorm in Amherst. She signed up for a semester of classes at U Mass. Soon she was studying art history, costume design, American literature. She got a part-time job at a bookstore in town and dreamed of inhaling the books. At parties she met atheists and Communists and women who wanted to go to Paris to dance. Her roommate encouraged her to get her virginity out of the way and she did just that, coupling up with a man at a party with a red corduroy jacket and sideburns. When she woke up the next day, with blood on her sheets and her head throbbing, she thought she was sick from all the vodka punch he had brought to her the night before. Instead there was a speck of light in her belly.

I was born nine months later. She named me Margaret Evangeline to appease her Catholic parents and had me baptized in their hill town parish.

I was Maggie from the start. My mother never saw the guy again or even knew his story. She said she kept expecting to run into him at some strange moment – glancing up from her coffee in the cafeteria or walking across campus through a light snow – but the image never materialized. My father was a phantom.

My mother had hoped to continue with her studies but with a small child and parents who now saw college as a corrupting force, she had no choice but to quit and get a job. Soon she was waking up at first light and driving her Dodge Dart to the parking lot of Gillette House at Smith College to mix pancake batter, boil eggs, and pour dry cereals into plastic dispensers. Once the breakfast rush was over, she would pat ground beef into burgers, make herb focaccia rolls, and toss greens together to serve the crowd again at noon.

My mother never married. It was just the two of us in a rental house on Summer Street, down the hill from campus. We had a nice life but we both dreamed of more. My mother was determined that I would get the education that she had abandoned. I was enthralled with the arts, taking every possible opportunity to be on the stage. In the end, we compromised. I got a nice financial aid offer from Barnard to study theater. A few months after I graduated high school, I got on a Peter Pan bus and motored towards my new life in New York.

I was intoxicated by the city. It had stood in my mind for years like Emerald City at the end of the yellow brick road. For my first few months, I was Dorothy without Toto.

I worked two campus jobs – one in the library, one in the bookstore—so I could buy theater tickets. On weekends I took the subway downtown to see *The Heidi Chronicles* and *Angels in America* and *Lips Together, Teeth Apart.* I drank cappuccinos in cafes on MacDougal, paging through my dog-eared copies of *A Doll's House* and *The House of Blue Leaves* and *Crimes of the Heart.* In campus productions, I played Nora and Bananas and Babe.

I begged my mother year after year to pay for me to get headshots. It was a huge financial investment and potentially a waste of money. But, eventually, we made a pact: if I stayed on course to graduate, she would buy me headshots as my graduation gift.

And so it was, with my diploma in hand, that I moved from campus to a small walk up on 13th Street, a newly minted graduate with a box of headshots and resumes to send to casting directors and agents. I spent my first year out of college slinging espresso and coming home to an empty answering machine.

One April day, the kind that only happens in the spring when you are young, I walked up to my fifth floor unit, unlocked the door, and saw that my answering machine light was blinking three times. My cat, Oswald, was on a litter box strike and I could smell astringent piss somewhere nearby. As I reached down with a paper towel to wipe up after him, I hit the button and my life changed.

"This is Cora Stuart, from the Cora Stuart Talent Agency. I would be interested in speaking to you about possible representation."

She left a number but I was screaming so I couldn't hear it. I scooped Oswald up into my arms and spun around. I had an interview with an agent. It was all I had ever dreamed of, that first step on the ladder to the sky.

And two months later I had an audition for a new soap called *Wild Hearts.*

Ian and I met at my first screen test, when the show was considering me for the role of Valentina Wilder. The studio was in Brooklyn, but the audition was in Manhattan at the offices of a company that cast for a variety of New York-based shows. In the lobby, there were pictures of all their famous productions: cop shows, sitcoms, soaps. I was nervous as hell. When I stepped into the audition room, there were only two people there, dwarfed by a big empty white room that resembled a dance studio. I walked over to an "X" marked on the floor. After a moment, the doors opened again and the most beautiful man I had ever seen entered. He looked like a young Elvis.

They asked us to do two scenes: a dramatic one and one that ended in a 10-second kiss. I had done stage kisses before but never with someone I had just met. When our lips touched, I was surprised to feel a flicker of his tongue in my mouth.

A few days later, Cora Stuart called me to say that the show liked me but not for the role of Valentina. I was being cast instead as Mira Thornton, an orphan who worked as a nanny for the younger Wilder kids. And the actor from my audition would be playing Mira's love interest Jacoby.

Soon we all slipped into our new roles. The show was taped in a huge, hulking building in industrial Brooklyn that looked like a chocolate factory.

Every day we convened there, sitting in barber chairs while make up was applied, running lines over cups of coffee, standing in camera blocking with curlers in hair and scripts in hand. We were there each day to create a world for viewers. When the cameras blinked red, we slipped into another reality, an inviolable realm like a snow globe. I was Mira, a blonde ingénue who had been hired to nanny the wealthy Wilder children. Ian was Jacoby, a bad boy with a criminal past, who had an illegal job tilling the fields at the Wilder vineyard. This was *Wild Hearts*, a daytime soap that ran for fifteen years before the Internet and reality TV killed it off.

The early days were heady. We were working actors in our early 20s, making $1000 a show and often working four days a week. After a few years, when the show was sold to foreign markets, we got monthly residual checks. I made in a month what my mother and I had lived on in a year in Northampton.

There were pressures, too. A lot of the actors on the show used pills and cocaine to curb their appetites. I refused and was always hungry. Learning four or five scripts a week was surprisingly demanding. Sometimes we worked past midnight only to have to turn around and be back on set at 7 AM. There was a relentless pace to daytime television, a strange mix of high demands and long periods of down time.

We fought, of course. The studio was in a grungy residential neighborhood with terrible deli food. We wanted sushi and fresh greens and better espresso, which required runs to faraway enclaves. There was all kinds of griping about shared dressing rooms. Actors often had their favorite make-up artist and their favorite dialogue writer. Coordinating all these particular requests while churning out five episodes must have been head spinning for the production assistants. When I think back on it, I am amazed at the grace some of the crew showed to us.

Ian was red meat and prop planes and Harleys with flames on their bellies. He was his cottage near the sound in Sea Cliff. He had never heard of Wordsworth or Salinger or even voted in a presidential election but I didn't care. I was just out of college, with my first acting gig, and I was enthralled with my co-star. When he offered me a ride home on his motorcycle, I never said no.

Ian lived in a cottage a stone's throw from the sound. His house was a dilapidated summer rental with mismatched furniture and a cracked skylight over the bed. He kept his TV in the basement. Some days he would drop the blackout curtains and we would curl up together to watch *Pulp Fiction* or *Goodfellas* or *The Godfather*. He would slip his thick fingers under my panties, fingering me while he stared blankly at the screen. We never made it to the end of a movie.

He liked music, too. He was a fan of classic rock like The Doors and the Stones as well as more recent indie artists like The Pixies and Nine Inch Nails. Some days when we got home, he would put "Where Is My Mind" on the sound system. The music would reverberate off the walls, forcing both of us into silent, rehearsed motion.

We had a standard routine. I wore a one-piece teddy, red or pink or sometimes black, and I got on my knees on his bed, which was always made immaculately. I would kneel there, rubbing my breasts slowly, until he appeared in the doorway. When I saw that he was erect, I would pull one of my breasts out and lean over to lick my nipple. He loved that part. He would slather lube over his cock and walk over to the edge of the bed.

He liked to fuck my breasts. I let him. I would slide down to the edge of the bed, pull my breasts out and press them around his cock into a soft vaginal passage. He would thrust and throw his head back when he came.

We did this a lot, always at his house, always at his direction, the first year we were on the show together. At the start of season two, he flew to Las Vegas with Jasmine Dakari, our co-star, and they married. I was blindsided, crushed. I got to spend their first year of marriage making out with her husband in front of the cameras. She got to hop on his bike and go home with him.

When I met Peter a few months later, at a beach weekend full of Ivy Leaguers, I fell into his arms. I was more than happy to leave Ian behind. When I got pregnant a few months later, it was blessing beyond measure. Peter and I married on New Year's Eve, my belly protruding slightly under my satin dress, and bought an apartment on the Upper East Side. I was a wife and mother. It was the life I had dreamed of.

But I never forgot about Ian. Not really.

CHAPTER THREE
NOW

THE PROFESSOR WAS a sturdy woman with long strands of blonde hair tied into a ponytail. She wore Converse high tops, cat-eye glasses, and wandered around the theater stage in circles, talking about Sylvia Plath and Gertrude Stein. At the end of her lecture she hit a button in her hand and a slide of Michelangelo's *David* appeared on the screen behind her.

She said, "If you don't break through your fear, the slab of marble never becomes a perfect naked man. So many people claim that they have a story in them. Do you?"

It was the end of the week and the lights in the darkened theater dramatically turned on with the last question. She had a student assistant in the lighting booth just for moments like these.

I was skulking in the back row, my hair up under a Jets cap that I had snagged from Riley's room on my way out of the city. I was at Ithaca College, in the humanities department, sitting in a summer session course called Ravenous Muses. The website listed it, taught by a woman named Esther Oden. How many could there in upstate New York? I hoped that I would be as unrecognizable to her as she was to me.

After the class ended, a few students approached her. She was chatting with them near the stage, nodding her head in conversation as I got closer.

Her attention diverted as I joined them. A young black guy with short dreadlocks and a Lucky Strike t-shirt was talking about Andy Warhol.

"We have another session starting up in a few weeks," she said to me, cutting the young man off. "Next week is finals for this one." Her voice had an edge to it, as if I were not welcome to join the conversation.

Who was it that said that acting is the art of making the unlikely seem plausible? Right now I was doing my best acting to convey that I hadn't heard the stern quality to her tone. The young man smiled at me sympathetically.

"I've decided on my final project. I'm going to write a paper on *A Raisin in the Sun*," he said to her as he pulled his backpack on and wandered away. The young woman standing with them, wearing jean overalls and ballet slippers, departed with him.

When they were beyond earshot, Esther said, "You think that cap is helping you? I know who you are. You have a lot of nerve showing up at my place of work."

"I just wanted to tell you that Ian is dead. He killed himself."

A cloud of emotion crossed her face. For a moment I saw her young face again, full of optimism, free of tension. "I'm not surprised," she said. "Now get the fuck out of my town."

I wandered through campus. The quad was alive with food trucks, students playing Frisbee, an outdoor art show. The artist had done a series of representational pieces about apple orchards in the region. The trees were heavy with fruit, dripping down like breasts full of milk. I pulled into my wallet and removed two fifty-dollar bills. I selected the one I liked best and bought it. I was still thinking about redecorating and thought this might be a nice addition to the living room.

I stopped by the college bookstore, raking a glance over the stacks. I asked the clerk behind the register if Esther Oden had published any works. He directed me to the "Of Local Interest" section. I scanned the titles, seeing local history and photography from the region. I paged through an ethnography on a local commune. It was called *Paradise Regained*: *An Oral History of Concordia, 1980-1989.*

Finally I settled on the one I was looking for. It was a chapbook of poetry titled *The First Time.* It had a vibrant yellow cover and embossed lettering. Apparently Esther was a poet. I paged through it and skipped to the final entry. It was called *Jesus at the Motel 6.*

A bed with fingers
Aqua diamonds shimmer
The highway outside is a river of sound
Those grassy banks
Tadpoles you drink
You're lost and I am found

I took the chapbook and the ethnography to the register and paid for them both. Then I asked the clerk for directions off the labyrinth campus.

❧

It was about three hours from downtown Ithaca to Page's house. She lived on a rural route up at the top of a small hill. I stopped at a grocery on the way. I had promised her a meal so I picked up two pieces of blue fish, some rice, a jar of marinara, and a bunch of fresh asparagus. I couldn't wait to strip down to my bikini, dip my toes in the pool, and numb out to a slushy drink.

As I turned onto Deer Path Way, I felt the familiar tingle of our annual girls' weekends. We had done this every year since Riley was a toddler and I always enjoyed it. Page's house was rustic, built by her own hands with money left to her when her father died. It was a glorified tree house with overstuffed furniture, piles of yarn, and more books than a person could read in a lifetime.

Page's red Saab was parked just under the carport. Her Labradoodle, Sunny, was pacing back on forth on the pine deck that fronted her property. I parked near the Saab and walked first around back, where there was a patio and beyond it, the pool. It was eight-thirty but Page already had her hanging lights on. There was music piped through the outdoor speakers. The Cocteau Twins' *Heaven or Las Vegas.* My favorite. She knew me so well.

Page and I had met for the first time during orientation week at Barnard. An RA was giving me a tour of the hall and stopped by the room I had been assigned. I entered and found an attractive brunette in a pink bra and matching panties, talking on the landline, a cigarette dangling from her lips. Barely registering my presence, she gestured to the plastic mattress on the other side of the room, the one near the windows that looked out onto Broadway. She had already made her own bed closer to the door.

We were both only children, but that was where the commonality ended. One night after a Columbia party our first year, still dizzy from vodka punch, Page confessed to me that her father was Barnaby Miller, the five-term Senator from Minnesota who had died in prison, discovered by a guard in his cell, strangled by the cord from a women's red silk robe.

"Son of a bitch couldn't even have a decent death," Page said to me. I remembered the late night comedy after it happened, the merciless jokes about a senator dying in women's clothing. "On the bright side," one of them had said, "Victoria's Secret has offered to pay for his funeral."

Page was brilliant, a shining star on a campus with plenty of competition. While I flailed around and eventually graduated with a 2.6, she would sit up nights on her bed, tapping quotes into her word processor and pacing around with a cigarette when the logjam thoughts wouldn't quite break free. By sunrise she had crafted a paper that would earn her top marks. Over the years her desk piled high with essays marked with professors' sycophantic comments, the same faculty who never knew who I was when I dropped by their office hours. "You're going to need to remind me of your name," a professor would say as he cleared off a seat opposite his desk. "You're in Romantic Poetry and Prose?"

When I asked her how she pulled it all off, Page said to me, "What do you think prep school is for? It's the art of an easy A."

After we graduated, she spent a few years club hopping in Manhattan, married and divorced the same man twice, and landed in a rustic house in Westchester paid for by her father's estate. Her days were a flutter of hot yoga, DIY projects, and sex parties. I was certain that one day our friendship would implode in a meltdown of buried resentments finally voiced, but it hadn't happened yet. She was the closest thing I had to a confidante.

I tried the sliding class door leading into the kitchen but found it locked. I peered into the window through the half-light of the kitchen and into her living room. Page was seated erectly on a chair. I waved when our eyes met. She jumped up and ran back to envelope me in a hug.

"I need a drink," Page said. "We both do." She got busy in the kitchen, crushing ice in the blender, squeezing limes, pouring orange liquor into a measuring cup. I unpacked the food I had bought and started our meal. I poured some olive oil into a pasta pan, dumped a half-cup each of white rice and marinara, and added a cup of chicken stock. I turned the flame low, washed the asparagus spears under the faucet, doused them in salad dressing, and put them on a platter with the flanks of blue fish. I joined Page outside, where she was firing up the Weber.

"Damn, what a week. I can't believe this news about Ian," she said, putting the lid down to hold in the heat. She handed me a large glass of frozen margarita. I drank it greedily. Page walked up the slope towards the pool.

I glanced at my watch. The rice would have to be stirred in eight minutes. I followed her up a slight incline and took a seat beside her at the lip of the pool. She had turned on the underwater lights. The water was ice cold. Bliss.

"So," Page said. "How are you feeling?" Page knew most of my sordid history with Ian, including my unresolved feelings for him.

"I don't think I'm feeling anything yet," I said. "That's part of the problem."

"It's sad," Page said. "He can't have been much over forty. Was it drugs?"

Julian had told me that Ian had drunk a few ounces of digitalis. The lab had found traces of it in a bottle of Vitamin Water. It was a natural poison that you could cultivate in your garden. The police had found a plant growing in Ian's yard.

"It's strange. Why go to all the trouble of growing a poisonous plant when guns are legal?" When I said nothing, Page said, "Sorry. I'm being morbid. When is the last time you saw him?"

I had a clear memory of the last day I had seen Ian. It was our final taping day about five years before. When we were finished with our last scene together, he found me in my dressing room. At this point, he had been married and divorced from our co-star Jasmine Dakari. She had left the show to film a police procedural on the other coast. I had been married to Peter for many years; Riley was twelve. Ian's and my romantic past was as untouchable as the fantasy we played in front of the camera. And yet I still had feelings for him, and I still felt emotional at the thought of never seeing him again.

"I got you something," he said, proffering a small blue velvet box. I opened it to find a gold charm with "J" and "M" intertwined.

"I figured you were going to take her charm bracelet, right?" He said. "Now you'll always have Jacoby and Mira with you."

I felt a prick of tears at the memory of this. I didn't want to talk about it.

"I need to get the fish on," I said, standing up. Once out of the water, the humidity hugged me from all sides.

"Hon, I'm sorry. Am I being insensitive?" Page followed me down the path to the patio. I slid open the door and pulled out the platter of food. Page went inside and refilled our drinks. I had finished my second by the time dinner was ready.

"So don't kill me," Page said as we served up our meal and took a seat at the table outside. "But Peter called here earlier. He was worried about you."

Well, that was a first. "We're splitting up," I told her, taking a bite of the blue fish. "I'm going to ask him to move out. I planned to do it when we got back but I've been overwhelmed."

Page paused with her glass aloft, considering this. "Mags, are you sure you know what you're doing? Riley just left home for college and you have just heard this shocking news about Ian. Now might not be the time for a major change."

"This wasn't a recent decision. I told him before we left for Italy that the trip was our last shot. This has been a long time coming."

"And?"

"And we didn't have sex in the most romantic place on earth. That aspect of our relationship has completely stalled."

There was part of me that hated telling my best friend these secrets. I didn't want to admit what I now believed to be true. I had failed at marriage.

"I think Peter is gay," I said, hoisting my glass to my lips.

Page gave me a dubious look. "He's not gay; he's just not attracted to you. There is a difference."

I gave her the evil eye.

"Don't misunderstand me, Mags. You're gorgeous. But an orgasm starts in the brain, not in the crotch."

"Your point is what?"

"You and Peter have huge mental hurdles. There were all your issues with Riley, for one."

I sat back in my chair, wishing there were more freshly made margaritas. Instead, I leaned my head back and looked at the night sky, which was fading from blue to black.

I thought of those days back on the set, me standing on my mark, the cameras rolling into place with Ian opposite me. His eyes were pools of soft brown. I wanted to lose myself in them. And I thought of the afternoons I would climb on the back of his Harley and ride with him to his cottage by the sound. He would turn on music and the base would reverberate off the walls. I would pull on a teddy and climb onto his bed, on my knees, the way he liked it.

Lying in bed under his cracked skylight, the night sky like this one above us, I was flush, curious, maybe a bit desperate. "Have you ever heard of shadow play?" Ian had said.

"Is that the band you're always talking about?" I said. Ian bellowed in laughter.

"No, little one," he said, using a term I never cared for. I felt like a child being mocked by an older sibling. "It's definitely not a band."

Sitting here now, I couldn't help but wonder if I had just let that conversation die that night, where we might all be today. Ian could be alive. Esther might be living a very different life than the one I saw today at Ithaca College. And where would I be? I might never have had Riley.

It was a strange hypothetical mix, too much for me after a day like today. I got up from the table, went inside, and closed the sliding glass door.

When I woke, it was pitch black. A light feather duvet covered my body. I reached through the oblivion, swatting left and right until my hand hit a sleek surface. I hit a button and my phone illuminated. 3:11. Wind rustled through the treetops outside my window. An owl screeched.

It was not unusual for me to wake at this time of night, especially if I had had a few drinks with dinner. At home in the city I just padded into the kitchen to drink some cold water or switched on the TV to keep me company. Here I felt somewhat limited in my options. I swung myself around and put my bare feet on the carpet. I could make out nothing in the darkness so I used my phone as a flashlight. Outside my door and down the hallway there was a bathroom. Page had forgotten to leave the light on.

I moved along hesitantly, unsure of my footing. The refrigerator downstairs was humming and when it cycled off, the canopy of dark seemed to expand. I ran my hand against the painted walls, hoping to hit a light switch.

There was a yelp and a wail and Sunny began barking on the first floor, a steady insistent howl. My heart accelerated and I stood like a statue in place, aware that something was downstairs. Sunny was panting insistently, her nails clicking back and forth on the kitchen tile. There was a loud creek from somewhere inside, feet on the floor, and a head beam of bright light.

"It's probably just a coyote," Page said as she hit the overheads and made her way down the wooden staircase to the first floor. She was gone for a bit, talking to Sunny until the dog's agitation became a whimper.

Page emerged up the stairs with two pint glasses of water.

"I'm parched for some reason," she said. "How much did we drink?" She handed me a glass and sipped from her own. "I'm surprised you didn't break a toe out here. I forgot to leave the nightlight on. You all right, Mags? You seem a little spooked."

I shook it off. "I'm just not used to the dark," I said.

When I woke again, sunlight was flooding my room. The aroma of coffee wafted through the air. A blender chuffed on and off. There was a low hum from a TV, a trained voice opining on some news event: a typhoon in Singapore, a political uprising in Bolivia, a new virus brought on a plane from West Africa.

"Hey sleepyhead," Page said as I descended the stairs. She was still sweating in her running clothes, chopping fruit on a cutting board. "Can I get you some coffee or a raspberry smoothie?" She took a long pull on her pint glass of ice water.

I shook my head and took a seat at the living room table. There was a tower of clementines at its center and the morning's *New York Times* still wrapped in blue plastic.

"I actually have to get back to the city," I said. "I have an audition."

Page walked over with her glass and took a seat. "Wow, big news. You didn't tell me that."

In the five years since the show ended, work had been scarce. At most I had one commercial and guest star audition a year. I hadn't booked anything in six months. My agent, Cora, had called me before I left for Italy to let me know that there was an open casting call for a play. I knew it was a long shot, but I was still willing to try. I missed performing.

"It's a Wendy Wasserstein play," I said. "*The Sisters Rosensweig.* They are doing a two-week revival at a theater on the Upper West Side."

"I remember that play," Page said. "It was big when we were at Barnard. Didn't she get the Pulitzer or something?" I remembered it, too. I had seen Madeleine Kahn and Jane Alexander in the original production. I was up for the role of Pfeni, the third sister in the cast, a globetrotting journalist who is dating a bisexual man.

"At least let me make you some breakfast before you leave," Page said. "I went to the farmers' market yesterday."

I sat back and let her get busy. It was nice having someone else care for me.

It was about an hour and a half back to the city, about what I expected given the time of the season and day. I blared The Doors as I drove. *Come on come on come on come on now touch me babe. What was that promise that you made? Why won't you tell me what he said? What was that promise that you made?* I loved the whiskey vocals and organ build.

As the hazy summer skyline came into view, I turned off the music and focused on getting home. Traffic slowed. Horns honked. The city rhythm led me back.

When I reached the parking garage near our building, the burly Russian worker waved me in. I parked in our spot and cut the engine. As I grabbed my overnight bag from the seat next to me, something dropped to the floor of the passenger seat. I swiped my hand down to the ground and pulled up a small piece of paper. It was an embossed business card. On the front there was a design and on the back there was a phone number. I held the card up to available light, fishing in my bag for my reading glasses. As I settled them on my nose, I saw that the image on the front was of two linked red circles. It resembled a figure eight turned on its side. My colorist had a tattoo on her wrist with the same design. What was it called? *An infinity circle.* On the back of the card was a local phone number. I didn't remember seeing the card in the car yesterday when I left the city but I couldn't be sure, so I pocketed it.

Later that night, on my way back from the audition, I ordered Japanese for dinner. We had a favorite place on Lex that delivered. When I got back home, Peter was in his office, talking to a client in Tokyo. I had long ago accepted my fate as an S&P 500 widow. Peter worked ten-hour days and many weekends as well. He loved the unpredictability of the stock market, the mad fluctuations, and being able to provide financial bounty to his clients. In another time and place, he might have been a high-stakes gambler.

Peter's father was the kind of man whose idea of quality parenting was allowing his son to eat the olive out of his Martini glass at the end of long workday. If they stood any chance of having a bond, it would be in the office. Peter joined his father's firm just after he graduated Cornell. They had worked together until Peter's father died of a massive stroke ten years ago.

I moved about the kitchen, opening a bottle of Stoli and a box of powdered sugar. I cut limes in half and squeezed them in a press. I dropped crushed ice into a shaker, measured vodka and juice and sugar, shook and served. I placed our glasses on the dining room table, next to a wooden platter with the sashimi and shaved ginger. I placed smaller bowls at either setting with a heap of rice and a serving of edamame.

Peter took a seat, gulping half his drink in a single shot. He popped open an edamame pod.

"Late night," I said absently, lifting my chopsticks and snapping them together.

"The markets will be closed for Labor Day so I'm trying to secure a few things before then," he said. "How was Page?"

"The usual," I said. "She told me you called her."

He ignored the comment so I barreled on. I handed him the business card I had found in my car earlier.

"Could this be something you picked up recently? I found it today." Peter drove our car more often than I did.

"I don't recognize it," he said. He dug into a pile of seaweed salad and sprinkled some soy sauce over his mound of steamed rice.

"There is an event next week on Wednesday night. Can you make it?"

"What is it?"

"A memorial," I said. "My co-star died."

"Anyone I know?" Peter said, wrinkling his nose. He had never hidden his disdain for the show. I'm not sure he had ever even seen a full episode. He told me often that I was too talented to be a soap actress.

"Ian Dorrit. You probably met him at a Christmas party once or twice."

Peter considered that while he swallowed. "Looked like a young Elvis? Wife looked like a young Cher?"

"A bit, yes. But they're divorced now. Have been for years."

"God, he died? He can't have been much over forty. Was it drugs?"

"In a way. Poison."

Peter's face changed from quizzical to somber. How many conversations had we had like this over eighteen years? My husband was only vaguely aware of what went on with me. He didn't know about Ian, or much about Page, or even much about his own son.

"I'm afraid I have to be in Boston next week. Please send my regrets."

I sized him up squarely. "Peter, this is kind of a big deal. I would like you to be there."

"And I would like to be there with you. But I have clients who are going to be in Boston for a few days. The Japanese business culture accepts no excuses. If I'm not there, I could lose this account."

I threw my chopsticks down. The clatter made him flinch.

"I'm not sure I want to be married anymore," I announced. I was surprised by the casualness of my tone. I had always expected a moment like this to be more dramatic.

He sighed and put down his glass. "So you've said, Maggie. Are we going to do this again?"

"I'm serious, Peter. We agreed to re-evaluate after Italy. This just isn't what I imagined from a marriage."

"Maggie, please. This relationship is not a menu. You can't just send something back if you don't like it."

"I feel like I am not important to you," I said.

"You're creating that," he said. "If things don't go your way, you decide what they really mean. You're lost in your own narrative."

"I want to be with a man who finds me attractive."

"Jesus, Maggie, you're a fucking actress. You're one of the most beautiful women I have ever seen. Why do I always have to validate your insecurities?"

"You are not attracted to me, Peter. We haven't had sex in months."

He flinched noticeably at this comment. His next remarks were chilly. "You think that's unusual at this stage in a marriage? I know a couple who hasn't had sex in five years."

"Really? Who?"

"You know Hayes Wilson? My client in Telluride? He told me he and his wife have slept side by side for five years. Not once. Nada."

"And you think they're happy? They don't deserve better?" I was imagining how this conversation had taken place between Peter and his client. Were they trading stories about midlife dry spells?

"My mother warned me about you," Peter said. "Before our wedding, she said you had had no role model for marriage and you wouldn't know how to ride out the rough patches. She could see something that I couldn't." This was rich coming from Justine, a woman who maintained a long marriage by never talking about anything personal with her husband.

"Your poor mother," I said. "Remember that dinner party when I embarrassed her by not knowing that Yale didn't admit women until the late '60s?"

"You asked my great-aunt if she went to Yale. I think most people there were embarrassed for you."

There had been so many moments like this over the years with Peter's parents. He never defended me. At a certain point, I don't think it even mattered what I knew. It wasn't about passing some test. Because of where I came from, I would never belong.

"So it sounds like we're in perfect agreement. This isn't a good match. Your mother was right."

Peter seemed weary, tired. We had traveled this loop many times and always ended up in the same place.

"You want me to move out? Is that what you're saying?"

"Yes."

"Fine. I'll have Samara book me an executive suite. I can move in after I get back from Boston." He pushed back from the table with force and left the room. I sat in the quiet until I heard him go to bed.

CHAPTER FOUR
THEN

THEY SAY THAT when you become a parent, you forgive your own mother. I did not find this to be the case. After Riley was born, it was harder for me to understand the parental indifference that had shaped my childhood. Before I had him, I told myself that my mother had been robbed of her own future when she found herself pregnant at nineteen. I was a constant reminder of what she had been denied: a college degree, a career, maybe the right companion.

When Riley was born, I was enthralled. I marveled at his ethereal stillness, his fine round head, his perfectly formed fingernails. For the first few months, he fit snugly in my arms, like a puzzle piece snapped in place. I drank in his smell, soothed by his gurgles and sighs. As the months neared a year, he developed basic language clusters, and I kept count of his words. There was nothing that thrilled me more than seeing him toddle into my bedroom at first light, climbing up onto the bed for a morning snuggle.

When I recounted all these details to my mother on our weekly phone calls, she met them with a vague bemusement. She seemed to regard me as a kind of pageant mother, with a pedestrian fascination with the quotidian. At some point it occurred to me that she might never have felt about me the way I felt about my son. As I watched Riley grow, I felt a creeping resentment of my own mother. I was determined that my child would never feel about his mother the way I did about mine.

It was possible, I suppose, that my mother was picking up on some of the tension in my marriage and judging my behavior because of that. So much is said about the damage an unhappy home does to a child. I think in our case it was the opposite. As Peter and I retreated from each other, Riley got all my love.

Early on, when things were difficult but not impossible, Peter and I went to see a couples' counselor. She was in private practice on Bank Street in a stately red brick building. Her waiting room had a library lined with art and travel books. Her office was tan and brown with the bearing of a university president's office. During our sessions, Peter and I sat side by side on a leather couch while she sat opposite us, nodding along to our comments like a marionette moving its head in time to a puppeteer.

She was always impeccably dressed with hair and make up that seemed professionally done. She would sit with one toned leg crossed over the other, secretly judging us I'm sure. I had once heard an interview with a therapist who said he could usually tell within a few sessions whether the couple had a shot of surviving. I was certain this woman had an opinion on this that she wasn't telling us.

In one session, Peter and I were bickering about how absorbed I was in Riley, who was six at the time. "I feel like I am my son's rival," Peter said. I was having no part of it. I accused him of caring more about himself than our child. After a pause in our disagreement, the therapist looked at us both squarely and said, "There is a difference between loving your child and being a good parent."

The comment stung. We were mutually repelled by the brazenness of her stern judgment. We deemed her unworthy of our intimacies and never went back.

In our worst moments, Peter had accused me of loving Riley more than I loved him. How could I deny something that was true? My son came to me with a purity that no man could ever contend with. It wasn't a fair fight. Of course I loved Riley more. Why did Peter have a problem with that? It was the nature of things.

But, of course, it was more complicated. After we met, Peter and I fell in love quickly and without much thought. His mother, Justine, was a Smithie and she was delighted to see her son with someone from that world. In the early days, she invited me over for lunch at their brownstone near the park. She would serve me an Arnold Palmer and a Chinese chicken salad and we would talk all afternoon. We liked the same plays and had read many of the same authors. She feigned interest in the show, burying her disdain for low art in diplomatic comments about the plotting and performances. She confided a family tragedy: Peter had had a sister who died when she was seven. Maude was a second grader, walking home from school with her nanny at Christmastime, when a taxi gunned through a yellow light and plowed down a crowd of pedestrians. Maude and her nanny were instantly killed. Peter was too young at the time to feel the loss, but Justine and Stuart were so anguished that they vowed never again to see another New York Christmas. They had stuck to it, too: every year since, the family flew to one location or another to avoid the holidays. Every year until Justine died, Peter and I would pack up Riley and take off through choppy air to some far flung tropical rental to spend a few weeks with Justine and Stuart, where we would sip pineapple rum and go body surfing, talking about anything and everything but Maude.

I resented Justine's steely control but I was in no position to challenge it. She was an MD in private practice; her husband ran a well-known investment firm on Wall Street. I was aware that my working class origins meant I had less say in how things were done. I accepted it, for a time.

What hurt me, though, was that Justine took so little interest in Riley. I had expected him to be smothered with love by her when he arrived, but for his first few years she was too busy to be involved. She was always immersed in writing a paper, or attending a conference, or chairing a gala. I told myself that I just wasn't accustomed to the schedules of accomplished women, but the indifference stung. When we saw the marriage counselor, she suggested to me that maybe it was too painful for Justine to be around a mother and child. I wanted to be empathetic.

Was it possible that I had neglected Peter intentionally, maybe as payback to his mother for her cold treatment of Riley? I didn't have an answer to that. When Justine died a few years before Stuart, I could never sympathize with Peter's losses. Justine and Stuart had never felt like family.

I had wondered over the years, though, if this disparity said as much about my marriage as it did about my love for my son or my ambivalence for my in-laws. Would I have felt differently if I had married a man I was truly passionate about? I thought of people I knew whose mothers ran off with lovers, abandoning them as vulnerable stages. Had they found a love that had eluded me?

CHAPTER FIVE
NOW

WITH PETER GONE for a few nights to Boston, I hired a moving service to come by to take his things to his new place while he was away. The apartment shrunk a bit as a few boxes and pieces of furniture disappeared. It occurred to me that our breakup had endured several stages: the first when we stopped having sex, the second when we went to Italy as a last resort. Now with his missing possessions transforming our shared space into something new, I had begun to feel single for the first time in years.

As I processed all this, I was grateful to have Ian's memorial to distract me. It was being held at 7 at a chapel in the village. The cast was meeting first at Julian's apartment for a drink. I hadn't seen any of them in the nearly five years since *Wild Hearts* was cancelled.

As my taxi glided through the streets, my past crowded around me. I had reached an age where I had a memory on nearly every corner of this city. Churches reminded me of weddings we had been to, theaters reminded me of nights out, department stores and shops reminded me of Christmas and birthdays. There was an art deco building on 27th and Madison where I had auditioned for the show, thrilling when I got a call back a few days later. There was a nightclub housed in a church with a gold onion dome where we had had a cast Christmas party one year.

When my driver reached the village, I felt a buzz of nostalgia. I had lived here for a few years after I graduated but only occasionally returned. Being here now felt like my youth had slipped into the vinyl seat next to me.

The driver turned onto Barrow Street and pulled over. I walked the half-block to Julian's building. In the lobby, there was an extra wide silver set of elevators. Taking one to the top floor, it felt like a slow moving room. Julian answered her door and grabbed me in an awkward hug. She was wearing her signature rockabilly shirt and porkpie hat and large, black-rimmed glasses.

"You're the second one here," she said in her staccato Bronx cadence. The interior of her place had polished blonde wood floors, hanging halogen lights, and paintings every few feet on the white walls. It reminded me a bit of an art gallery. There was a dining room table that sat six and an area near the far windows with couches and a coffee table. We were high enough to have a view of the Hudson. A hallway off the kitchen led to bedrooms. As far as I knew, Julian lived alone.

We made small talk while she poured me a glass of pinot grigio and herself a tumbler of cranberry juice over ice. Outside she had turned on her hanging lamp strands that lined the perimeter of her roof garden. I could see a man standing out there, dressed in black, inhaling a cigarette.

"I'll go say hello," I said and left with my drink. Ty Harris was standing near the edge of the roof. He had played Mira's first husband, Joshua Wilder, on the show. The fans had been outraged when Mira left Jacoby and went back to Joshua only months after she had stood him up at the altar in that oft-mentioned "Arabian Escape" episode. Somehow I had always liked the plotline, though. Mira's choices reflected her own chaotic background.

I embraced him warmly. "It's been too long," I said.

Ty had a bulky, sturdy build and black, untamed hair. I recalled from some of our love scenes that he was quite hairy underneath his linen. He had a thick tongue too. Mira and Joshua had made out plenty.

"I just heard the news. I was filming a commercial in London and Julian called me."

I couldn't remember the last time I had seen him. Our storylines had diverged after the first few seasons and we had drifted apart. He was a nice guy, but with little in common beyond the show, the friendship had faded away.

"How are your kids?" I asked him. I couldn't recall what their names were.

"Great. Marley is about to start her sophomore year at Smith and Asher his junior year of high school."

"Your daughter is at Smith. You know, I grew up in Northampton."

'I thought I remembered that," Ty said. "Didn't your mother work for the school?"

"Yup. Forty-two years in Dining Services. She's still there. And Sara? How is she?" His wife was a vivacious strawberry blonde with a knockout body who seemed a little ill at ease around the cast.

"She's fine. But we got divorced. She went back to Chicago with Asher. She never liked it here."

Our conversation was interrupted by the arrival of Corey Broderick. He sauntered over, looking every bit as adorable as I remembered him. He had a compact body and a mop of brown curls and huge eyes that made you believe again in good things.

Corey had grown up on a houseboat in the Louisiana Bayou, running down the slatted docks to get to the school bus in the morning. When he was sixteen, his mother came home and found Corey snuggling with a boy from the glee club. She gave her son a hundred-dollar bill and told him to get a bus ticket to "someplace that you are welcome." Corey hitchhiked to the French Quarter and only returned to his hometown a few years later when he heard his mother had died. After her memorial he rummaged through her belongings, returning with a steamer truck full of clothes.

"This town has nothing on NOLA tonight," he said, fanning himself and wiping some flop sweat into his hand. "You think Ian opened up the gates of hell just for us?"

I was a bit taken aback by his bluntness. Ian and Corey had never gotten along, but this hardly seemed like the time to bring it up.

"You look good, Maggie," he said, checking me out. I was wearing a black sheath dress and sling back sandals. I had pulled my hair into a loose chignon. Corey turned to Ty. "And you too, my friend."

"I'm sorry to be morbid," Ty said, stubbing out his cigarette while exhaling a last plume. "But do you know anything about Ian's death? It's a real shock. I don't think I fully absorbed what I heard the first time."

"Julian told me he poisoned himself," I said. "They found traces of digitalis in a water bottle near the scene. He had been growing the plant in his garden. Apparently just a few ounces can kill you."

"That's very Miss Marple," Corey said, taking a sip from his highball. "You think Ian set up a dramatic death to get his name in the papers?"

If he had, it didn't seem to be working. I had been Googling his name since I got back from Italy and he wasn't getting much coverage, just a few line items in the rags and some stories on gossip blogs. Every actor's dream is to trend on Twitter upon his demise, but that hadn't happened yet as far as I could tell.

Veruca St. Clair joined us, giving us all a sullen hello. She had always been a strange bird. Her raven black hair, streaked with deep purple strips, was tied up into a messy bun on her head. She was wearing Camper boots and a Betsey Johnson dress, which revealed skinny arms with a full sleeve of tattoos. I was mesmerized by the image on her left arm of a skeleton reaching its spindly fingers around a crystal ball. The woman was a walking art show.

"Does anyone want to get high?" she said, removing a small pipe from her purse. We all shook our heads. Veruca's father was a sculptor who had died of a heroin overdose when she was a child. It was possible this memorial was bringing that back.

We stood around awkwardly as she took a deep inhale. I surreptitiously waved away the smoke, not wanting to show up at a funeral smelling like weed.

"God, I hate funerals," she said. "Everyone lies."

Corey chuckled. "At my mother's service, everyone was trying to tell me what a good woman she was. I just wanted to scream in their faces, *she kicked me out of the house when I was sixteen. Do good women do that?*"

I glanced over at Ty and smiled wanly. This was getting raw much sooner than I had expected. Ty was the kind of guy who always saw the best in everyone, less for honorable reasons than a desire to not get deep and messy.

Julian came out and joined the group."Veruca is going to lead the way to the chapel," she said, linking arms with her. "We can walk there easily, right?"

I wasn't sure what the relationship was between these two. Years ago Veruca had been the writer's assistant and later she edited scripts. She was a pretty unpleasant person, even to the talent, which made me think she must have a connection to Julian that allowed her to keep her job. They appeared to have stayed in touch in the years since the show ended.

The five of us moved slowly through the languid August heat, making generic chitchat at appropriate lulls. The chapel was a few blocks over from Julian's place. It was small, with a brown exterior and white wooden pews inside. There were paintings of saints and icons and a domed roof over a simple altar.

We took seats near the front. It was already nearly full. The first two rows were reserved for Ian's family. I fanned myself with the program and then opened it to read his biography. It talked of cross-country solo flights, a love of steak and Jack Daniels, an unfulfilled desire to star in a Tarantino film. There was a black-and-white photo of him on the front, sitting in a relaxed pose on a deck somewhere. He seemed more peaceful and happy than I remembered him.

I thought of Ian as I knew him, sliding behind the wheel of his Porsche and cranking up the Def Leppard as he drove us home for a night in Sea Cliff. He was beautiful, cocky, inscrutable. No amount of fucking ever got me closer to knowing him. He remained a stranger to me.

Music swelled and a small group of people emerged from a room near the sacristy. Ian's father looked like Ian would have if he had traded in a diet of egg whites and protein powder for Dunkin Donuts and ribs. His sister was an attractive blonde with the svelte figure of a runway model. There were other family members with them too: teenage cousins who were genetic variations of Ian, a few older women who resembled Ian's sister.

A priest spoke for a few minutes, and then a few of Ian's friends. At the midpoint, the music swelled and Jasmine Dakari made her entrance. She was draped in a gorgeous purple dress that nicely offset her flowing black hair. She tapped the microphone playfully and then belted out a torch rendition of "Sweet Child O' Mine." It was one of Ian's favorite songs. Jasmine had undeniable stage presence. Once I had hated her. She was my personal and professional rival. Today, I was thankful that I could have this moment of grace to enjoy her gifts.

After the service, we all loitered for a bit before walking downstairs to a reception in the church hall. A long table was filled with Bundt cakes and platters of cookies and brownies. There was a large silver samovar at the end with stacks of coffee cups and saucers surrounding it.

I spoke briefly to Ian's father and sister, who greeted me with the blank emotions of strangers who have a friend in common. When Julian cut in to chat with them, I wandered off in search of the ladies' room. The church hall was surprisingly labyrinthine given the small size of the chapel. I eventually found a bathroom near the street entrance on the next floor.

As I was washing my hands the door squeaked open. Veruca was standing there.

"Who knew Ian had so many friends," she said, walking over and pulling a silver lipstick case out of her purse. She took a position next to me and began applying red to her thick lips. "I always thought he was a prick."

"And yet you're here, Veruca, so what does that say?"

She gave me a knowing glance, mirror image to mirror image. "I'm surprised that Esther isn't here. Did someone think to tell her?"

I was nonplussed by this reference. "How do you know Esther?"

"I don't," Veruca said. "Not really. I mean, I was her intern coordinator way back when but we were never close. But I kept running into her and Ian over the summer near Sea Cliff. I guess they were having a thing."

I turned to Veruca, face to face. "You saw Ian and Esther together recently?"

"Several times. I was staying with my friend over the summer. There is this breakfast place called Dottie's that all the locals hang out at. I saw them there a few times."

"You're sure it was the same Esther? The intern?"

Veruca scoffed. "Do you think I'm just randomly speculating for chuckles? We had several conversations. She told me all about her life up in Ithaca. She and her ex-boyfriend run a bookstore. She lectures at the university sometimes. She has a kid, you know."

I knew only one of these things.

Veruca stuck her lipstick case back in her purse and turned to exit.

"By the way, that creepy homeless actor is in the atrium. He was asking for you."

I exited after her and stood for a second in the half-light. I felt thick serpentine arms wrap themselves around my torso and a hot tongue in my ear. Someone was biting my earlobe.

"I've been wanting to do this all night," he said. His stubble felt rough against me as I pulled away. I could smell vodka on his breath.

"Jesse" I said, trying to maintain my composure. "What has gotten into you?"

He reached over and kissed me, pushing his thick tongue into my mouth. When I pulled away, he said, "The first one was so good. Will there ever be another?"

Jesse Jacobs had played Ian's brother on the show, a recurring character that showed up from time to time to do supporting scenes. For the first few seasons, Jesse slept in a beater van outside the studio, a remnant from his struggling actor days. I don't know that he was ever actually destitute. It was just part of his method.

I pushed him away, repulsed, and walked swiftly back to the reception hall. Julian, Veruca, and Jasmine were standing together near the samovar.

I gave Jasmine in a brief hug. "How are you holding up?"

"I think I'm in shock," she said. Her earrings were gold and pearl and reminded me of chandeliers. "But I knew his family had a history of depression. It's why he never wanted to have children."

The comment hung in the air while the conversation stalled.

Over her shoulder, I saw Jesse piling up his plate from the dessert bar. He had a tower of lemon squares. I wondered what had happened to him since the show ended. It was possible he was still living in his van.

"Who invited Jesse?" I asked.

Julian shrugged. "He and Ian used to party together. I figured Ian would want him here."

Years ago, after Ian and I broke up but before I met Peter, I had slipped into that beater van one night and fucked Jesse Jacobs. I was drunk and depressed and wanted to feel attractive to someone. Until tonight, I assumed he had forgotten about it. Or maybe I just hoped that he had.

Corey found me as I was eyeing the dessert table. "We're going to cut out, go back and chill at Julian's," he said. "You in?"

I grabbed a Russian teacake and popped it into my mouth. The powdered sugar sprinkled down my dress. "I'm in," I said.

Soon the same group was meandering back towards Julian's loft. Jesse and Jasmine had joined us. When we got back to the roof, Julian pulled seven deck chairs into a circle and lit a few candles. She uncorked a bottle of pinot grigio. Veruca lit a joint and passed it around. We were all more receptive now that the service was over.

"It's strange when someone young dies," Veruca said. "My father was only forty-seven. It feels like time has been stolen from them."

"He lived well, though," Julian responded. "Many people don't accomplish in twice the time what he did in forty-two years."

"It's because of the tree tops," Jesse said. "He died because of the tree tops."

There was an awkward pause. No one was quite sure what to make of his words. Back when we were on the show, I was never sure if his babbling, incoherent personality was a put-on. Now that he was no longer acting, it seemed more authentic.

Jesse reached into his jeans pocket and pulled out a scrap of paper. Ty reached over and diplomatically took it from him. He then passed it around. When it got to me, I saw that it was a handwritten note with the following words: *the trees were so high/ how have you seen us/ once you were mine/nothing between us*

"Where did you get this?" I said.

"At the viewing," he said. "Last night. When I walked by the coffin, this note was stuck inside. I think it was his suicide note."

So Jesse had taken a souvenir from the casket. Somehow, I wasn't surprised.

"There was a viewing last night?" I asked him.

"Only close friends and family," he said. I guess none of the rest of us qualified.

I began to feel a bit uncomfortable so I got up and cleared away empty wine glasses.

"Just leave them in the sink," Julian said. She had followed me in while the rest of the group sat outside. I turned to her.

"I need to cut out," I said. "Everything is hitting me all at once."

It was a lie. My mind was swimming with a memory I had of Ian. I wanted to be alone to process it. One day at the cottage, when we were lying in bed, he told me that as a boy, he liked to climb trees in his backyard. He could get up so high that people were the size of dolls on the ground. One day, when he was way up in the branches, he saw his mother slip out onto the patio. She walked around, cutting flowers from the garden with clippers, arranging them in a basket. While he watched her from above, his father's truck pulled into the driveway. A door slammed, and his father's voice rose in anger. His father appeared, bellowing, and stalked over to his mother. Ian's father struck his mother, sending her and the cut flowers scattering to the ground.

Ian told me that he stayed in the tree that day until it got dark. He was immobilized by the fear he felt. When he climbed down, the moon was high in the sky. He slid the patio door open. He found his father asleep on the couch. The house was quiet.

Ian never saw his mother again.

CHAPTER SIX
THEN

Ian and I had been sleeping together for about five months when he raised the issue of shadow play for the first time. We were lying in his bed, looking up at the night sky through a skylight over his bed. I was naked, trailing my hand across his torso, feeling flush. "Have you ever heard of it?" He asked me. I hadn't. At that point, I was twenty-three and was fairly inexperienced.

Shadow play, Ian explained, went like this: a couple made the acquaintance of someone they wanted to do a threesome with. For clarity, you could call this person The Shadow. Once selected, The Shadow would be given a set of house keys and three pre-selected dates and times. On one of those nights, The Shadow would enter the house when it was empty, hide in the bedroom closet, and wait for the couple to come home. At an appropriate moment, when the couple was in the act, The Shadow would come out of the closet and join them. The appeal of this game was the element of surprise: you never knew which night the Shadow would be present.

"So it's like a watching game? You never know which night you are being observed?"

"Exactly," Ian said. "And it's so fucking hot. Are you game?"

I was nervous, unsure. It seemed risky to me. Although I had no knowledge of what he did when I wasn't around, Ian and I were starting to act like a twosome. I didn't want to share him with another woman.

Sensing my reservations, Ian leaned over and kissed me lightly. "I'll let you pick the third. You're in control, baby."

I said nothing.

"Will you think about it?" Ian said, his voice tender. "I'd really like to share this experience with you."

I told him I would consider it. I tried to sound open-minded, but the truth was that I didn't think I could ever enjoy it.

I knew better than to suggest a man to be our shadow. Ian was a red-blooded Kinsey zero. He could have never gotten it up for a guy. So over the next few weeks, I began to look at my female co-stars sidelong, wondering if any of them would have been willing to do this.

Ian had spelled out the process: once I selected my person, I should invite them out for a drink or coffee and create a pleasant space to introduce the idea. Consent was key: no one should feel pressured. A simple "no" meant the end of the discussion along with a request to keep the conversation private.

At some point in my deliberations, I began to notice Esther Oden. After our first meeting at Absinthe, she had followed up with Veruca and secured a summer internship on the set. I had seen her around, bringing sandwiches and coffee onto the set for the actors or standing in line at a photocopier in the production office. She was sweet, with a warm smile and rolling laugh. I could tell she was doing well with her duties and was probably on the short list to secure a job after she graduated the following year.

She was also dumpy, with large breasts that overwhelmed her small frame. Her face was plain, dominated by a pair of clunky glasses. She was overweight, with a body that showed visible signs of indulgence.

As the weeks went by, and I felt the sting of Ian's boredom with our regular routine, I settled on her as my choice. There was no way Ian would be interested in her outside the bedroom, so I felt a giddy freedom in my selection.

I befriended her, stopping by the writers' office to idly chat with her about Barnard and the latest summer movies. I could sense that her fandom of the show was waning. It was inevitable: long days on the set killed the fantasy for all of us. But I could tell she still liked Ian. This would be a nice little gift for her to take home for senior year.

One afternoon, I invited her out for coffee. The neighborhood near the studio was starting to be gentrified and a hipster coffee place had opened up a few blocks away. We set a time and I made my way over there when I had a break. Esther had agreed to meet me when she was done for the day.

There was a garden out back with seating. Speakers piped music in. I took a seat on a bench and wrapped my hands around my coffee cup. I took a sip. I had read somewhere that hot beverages actually help a person cool down. It was warm today but not oppressively so.

I was nervous as I waited and more so when Esther arrived. She joined me in the garden with a glass of iced coffee with a spoon stuck in it. The milk hadn't been mixed yet and was curving and swirling in strange shapes like a lava lamp.

Sitting across from her, I appraised Esther like a piece of prime meat. She had the look of someone who had missed out on being beautiful by a random shake of the cosmic dice. If her parents' DNA had mixed just slightly differently, she might have been striking. But as it was, her features were a bit too broad and her skin too sallow. She could never be skinny enough to be accepted in show business.

Sitting that day in the pleasant sun of an empty Brooklyn coffee garden, I could not have foreseen the events that were to come in the next few weeks. I had not yet learned about my own limits and my capacity for self-preservation. If I had known what was to come next, I would not have agreed to Ian's idea. I would have walked away even if it meant losing him. I would have been a better person. Or so I tell myself now.

CHAPTER SEVEN
NOW

When I got back from the memorial, my apartment was dark. I turned up the dimmer switch in the foyer, standing for a moment in front of the gilded wooden Buddha that hung on the wall between Riley's room and the guest bathroom. Peter and I had bought it on our honeymoon in Thailand. What pretenders we were, bringing home a religious icon when neither one of us was a believer or even knew much about religion. In the early days, we were all about surfaces.

In the living room, I flipped through our vinyl collection, thankful that Peter had not asked to have the turntable moved to his new place. I found a copy of the *Cruel Intentions* soundtrack. There was a track I loved by Elisabeth Fraser. I put the needle on the groove and allowed her pure voice to fill the empty space around me.

I sank into the couch, allowing the music to wash over me. I wondered what the last music was that Ian heard. Does someone who is suicidal have a bucket list of sorts, experiences they wanted to have one last time before it was over? Was there a last song, a last meal, a last view? Did Ian take a final flight in his plane, knowing he would never do it again?

I was fortunate, I suppose. Even in my darkest moments, I had never once considered taking my own life. The thought of a permanent black curtain dropping was far more depressing than any reality I had to live with.

It occurred to me now that, despite our sexual intimacy, and the affection that came before and after, that in some ways I didn't know Ian all that well. He may well have been struggling and I didn't know it. Or maybe the years after the show had been difficult for him. Cora Stuart, my agent, had told me many times that there are about ten thousand speaking parts each year in film, television, and commercials and about as many actors vying for each slot. Ian had had remarkable success early on, landing a lucrative job. He was young and attractive. I didn't like to think about it at the time, but I was sure that he could have had nearly any woman he wanted. Perhaps that had changed at he neared forty. The show was gone and with it his main source of recognition. It's possible that the world was changing around him and he couldn't adjust to the downgrade.

But was this really enough to drive him to suicide? I thought of Corey's comment that the foxglove poison sounded like something out of Agatha Christie. I was beginning to feel a creeping doubt that Ian had taken his own life. Someone could have poisoned his Vitamin Water with digitalis and placed the leftover plant in his garden. It could have been someone I knew. I thought of the group of people who had just memorialized Ian with me. Could one of them be a killer?

Back from my yoga class, paging through the morning newspapers, my cell phone buzzed. It was a week after Ian's memorial and I was getting used to a new routine. I had found a two-hour class at a studio on Lex that I was attending each morning. Each day this week, I had woken up early, had breakfast, and headed over to be on my mat by eight. By the time I got back and showered, it was nearly lunchtime.

"Are you free tonight?" Jasmine Dakari said breathlessly. It sounded like she was walking at a steady clip down the street. I could hear a stream of traffic in the background. "Seeing you all last week made me miss what we used to have. I'm getting the gang together for dinner at my place."

"Sure, I don't have plans," I said. I was hoping that I would hear back from Cora today about my audition. It had been nearly two weeks and there had been no news.

"I'm so glad," Jasmine said. "I've just been so upset about Ian. And no one in my life seems to understand. I am excited to spend time with people who get it."

There is a theory that all you need to bond with others is a shared space and a shared schedule. This is why our best social connections form at school and work. It had happened for us years ago on the set, all the time together forcing an intimacy that wouldn't otherwise have existed. Now Ian's death seemed to be bringing us back together.

It's funny how the memory erases certain things. Until I saw her at Ian's memorial, I had forgotten that I used to like Jasmine. My feelings had been colored by what happened later. I had wiped out our first season together, when we were two actresses who killed time by chatting in the make-up trailer and making coffee runs on our breaks. We had a certain simpatico even without our mutual attraction to the same man. It was part of why their betrayal stung so deeply. I had cared about both of them.

Jasmine lived in Tribeca in a renovated loft. I felt slightly nervous, like I was prepping for a first date, as I got ready that evening. I grabbed a bottle of red wine to add to the festivities and left my apartment at six. From what I had gleaned at the memorial, Jasmine spent most of her time working in LA but maintained this residence as well.

As I arrived, Corey was standing on the street near a set of steps that led to a front door. Every few moments a red ember lit up as he inhaled. His character, a police detective named Olli, had been killed off in the eleventh season. Since he had died heroically saving my character from a psychopath, I had always felt somewhat guilty.

"Sweet thing," he said, enveloping me in a hug that lasted a good long time. "Good to see you again."

"Are we the first to arrive?" I said, raking a glance over the street. I was dressed in a blue camisole, jeans, and black sling back sandals. Corey was in jeans and a white t-shirt. The late summer heat hung low.

"I guess so. So what have you been up to since the memorial?"

After a few glasses of bubbly, I might open up to Corey about the current state of my affairs. As it was, I opted for a banal synopsis of the past few days.

"How about you?" I said by way of a wrap up. "I didn't get a chance to ask you about what you've been doing since you left the show."

"Just finished up last year with a tour of *Joseph,*" he said. Since leaving *Wild Hearts*, Corey had done several tours of *Joseph and the Amazing Technicolor Dreamcoat.* He was quite a good vocalist. "But I've booked nothing since then. I'm actually living at Jasmine's right now since she's been on the coast. The other coast."

Jasmine was one of the few actors from the show who had worked consistently beyond it. It felt like she had a guest shot on every other crime drama that filmed in LA. Sometimes I hated turning on the TV and seeing her. It was a stab to the gut. She was still drop-dead gorgeous with an appealing screen presence and a smoky voice that distinguished her from other pretty faces. While I fully understood her success, I privately resented it.

"Sometimes I just feel like picking up and going back to Louisiana," Corey said. "This is not an easy life."

"I hear you," I said. Six months ago, I had done a production of Tom Stoppard's *The Real Thing*. Other than residuals from *Wild Hearts'* foreign markets, it had been my only acting income in several years. I had built up enough money from the show to live comfortably, even without Peter's income, but fulfillment was much harder to come by. Mira and her world had been part of me and I missed them.

"Looks who's here..." Corey said, distracted by someone walking up the sidewalk. Ford Sather squinted in the half-light and walked over. He had the leathery skin and wary eyes of a man who had put a lot of hard living behind him. He was distinguished, with silver hair at his temples and piercing blue eyes.

"Greetings," he said, placing two large hands on either of our shoulders. It felt like we were getting a benediction from a priest.

Ford Sather had played Duncan Wilder on the show, the second son of the main family. Duncan was a Norman Bates type who spent a lot of time in the attic sewing women's clothing. He was obsessed with Mira and thought she was his live action doll. Duncan liked to dress up in Jackie O sunglasses and a black wig and stalk young women around the family vineyard. Early on, Duncan had been obsessed with Mira. There were many episodes with him in the family attic, surrounded by bolts of colorful silk, sewing dresses for Mira on an old Singer machine. To his credit, Ford sold these scenes and gave them a poignancy that the writing did not. He was a fan favorite because of the humanity he brought to the role.

"It's good to see you again, kid," Ford said, enveloping me in a hug. When our cheeks touched, his stubble felt like sandpaper. "Sorry I missed the memorial."

"You still in the city?" I asked.

"Nope, I came down last week. I'm bunking right now with Ty. He sends his regrets. He couldn't make it tonight. I actually live upstate now."

The three of us moved up a set of stairs to a large black door. After a moment, Jasmine appeared. She greeted me warmly, taking both of my shoulders in her hands and kissing me on each cheek. She ushered us up a set of wooden stairs to the second floor. Her living room had Tuscan red walls, which led to an island in her kitchen decorated with a multi-colored mosaic, and a farmhouse sink and dual range.

"Gorgeous place," I said.

"I'm never here," she replied. "I've been working so much in LA that this place is pretty much vacant. Unfortunately I've hit a dry spell. I should be here for the next few months. Can I fix you something? A Cosmo? A Gimlet?"

"Sidecar?" I said, hit by an unapologetic desire to get sloshed. In the unlikely event that I had nailed my audition, I had time to work it off before the play started.

While the guys went out on the balcony to take in the view, I lingered near the kitchen watching Jasmine pull together the drinks ingredients. After a few minutes of shaking and stirring, she proffered a yellow drink with a sugar rim in a Martini glass. I took it gratefully. She began swaying to the music, turning it up a bit with a remote. The song was "California Girls" by Katy Perry. When the chorus hit, she belted out the lyrics.

Unsure of how to have a conversation with a woman who was now singing, I wandered around admiring the artwork on the walls. There were photographs of Parisian rooftops, a blue door in Fez, and family wedding photos. There was a portrait of her with two lookalike sisters, all three of them wearing black turtlenecks.

Jasmine sidled up next to me. "I love that photo," she said, noticing where my gaze was focused. "It was taken at my grandparents' farm in Ojai."

"You grew up in Southern California?" I had forgotten her basic biographical details.

"We did; mostly in the area around Malibu Canyon. Our father worked in the industry. He was a writer for a couple of sitcoms."

She boogied back and got busy in the kitchen, pulling salad plates out of the fridge and placing them at table settings. She continued until every seat had the same: a heap of greens with a few wildflowers on top.

We took our places. Jasmine and Corey sat at the head and base of the table; Ford and I were across from each other in the middle. We munched silently on our salads for a few moments. The music had changed to trance. I took a hearty gulp of ice water. I still felt buzzed from the sidecar.

"My acting coach asked me an interesting question recently," Jasmine said. "What has surprised you most about your life?"

"What did you say?" Corey replied.

"I thought I'd ask all of you before I tell you," she responded, taking another sip of red wine.

"I think resilience," Corey said. "I have been through some difficult times but I have always found reason to be optimistic. I don't believe in God per se, but I have been amazed at the strangers who have helped me along the way."

We all paused respectfully before he continued. "When my mom kicked me out, I had nothing. I hitchhiked to New Orleans not even knowing my way around. Fortunately I knew to go to a gay bar. I met this woman there that I called Auntie. She let me sleep on her couch for six months, helped me find a job. There have been people like that in every dark stage of my life."

"I'd probably say something similar," Ford said. "My mom died when I was thirteen. My biological father was a dick but his brother took me in. I had a much nicer childhood with him than I would have otherwise. I was amazed that anyone could be so kind with no discernable upside. He just was a good man."

My answer felt shallow in comparison but I offered it anyway. "I've been the most surprised by motherhood," I said. "Before Riley was born, I was not interested in children. But when he was born, I was just fascinated by him. He opened up a whole new world. I can't tell you how many

Pokémon characters I can name or football games I've watched. I liked them because he liked them."

"Kind of like when you have a crush on someone, and suddenly you're interested in everything they are," Jasmine responded.

"It's very much like that," I said. I wondered if she had ever wanted children. She probably had some options left. "How about you?"

"Well, it's funny. I told the class that what surprised me most about my life was the cyclical nature of things. When Ian and I broke up, I thought it was really done between us. I couldn't imagine ever finding him attractive again. But earlier this year he called me. Enough time had passed that I found myself really enjoying him again. We even briefly got back together. It's something I never would have imagined. But then I got another offer in LA so it had to end. But what I told the class was that life has a way of bringing people back in ways you never would have imagined."

"Amen to that," Corey said, holding his glass up. We clinked to our surprising reunion.

"Enough with all the deep thoughts, should we play 'never have I ever'?" Jasmine asked playfully. There were a few groans across the table but no actual objections. "You know how it works, right? Make a statement of something you have never done. Don't take a sip from your cup. Then everyone around the table who HAS done it has to take a sip from their own glasses."

We had all played this juvenile game at some point. I took my water glass in hand gamely.

"Let me open another bottle of wine," Jasmine crowed, jumping up. She stuck a corkscrew in the bottle of red I had brought and poured four glasses.

"Me first!" Corey said. He held his wine glass aloft without drinking from it. "Never have I ever slept with a woman." I watched Ford reach immediately for his glass and take a hearty swig. I paused and then took a timid sip myself. Corey's mouth dropped open. "You've been holding out on me."

There was some laughter and then the next person went.

"Never have I ever slept with twin brothers," Jasmine said, giddy at her comment. Corey took a sip. Everyone at the table guffawed. "Bitch!" Corey screamed.

"That revelation needs some follow up," I said, but Corey ignored me.

"Never have I ever sucked cock," Ford said, holding his glass in front of him. Corey, Jasmine, and I drank.

I had waited until last because I wasn't quite sure what I wanted to reveal or find out. I was buzzed and nervous, emboldened and fearful. How well did I even know these people? While the group waited, Jasmine divided the rest of the wine bottle into our glasses.

"Never have I ever stayed married forever," I said. Nobody drank.

Corey broke the silence. "You and Peter broke up?"

"Yes, I asked him to move out. He's staying elsewhere."

I wasn't sure if I was projecting, but no one seemed terribly surprised at the news. Jasmine went back into the kitchen to dish up the second course. It was a baked pasta casserole with fresh tomato sauce and basil. I eyed it greedily as she put plates down. Jasmine stepped over to the kitchen island and returned with another bottle of red wine.

She served us all some more with our pasta. Before we took our first bite, she raised her glass. We all joined her.

"To Ian," she said, and we all followed.

After the pasta, there was more wine and finally small bowls of lemon sorbet. I wouldn't have taken Jasmine for the domestic type, but everything had been delicious and presented with style. After we finished, she directed us to the balcony where we could sit and enjoy the nightscape. Soon, the four of us were sitting side by side, without words, drinking quietly. Ford flared up a joint and passed it along. I was the only one who declined. I didn't need any more encouragement to eat.

After the silence lingered for a while, Jasmine said, "When was the last time each of you saw Ian? I'd like to hear your stories."

We were all quiet for a moment.

"I saw him just a few weeks before he died," Corey said. "It was at a sex party. He had a girl in a swing."

I winced a bit at the thought. The others laughed.

Ford spoke next. "A few years after the show ended, one the directors had tickets to a 49ers/Patriots game. He called Ian and Ty and me and the four of us went. It was a freezing cold day. Ian flew us up to Foxborough in his private plane. It was the scariest landing of my life, by the way. We gave him hell for that. But the day was a blast."

I had a clear memory of the last time I had seen Ian. It was our final taping day about five years before. When we were finished with our last scene together, he found me in my dressing room. I wasn't sure I wanted to share it with the rest of the group. I let the others talk, instead.

When the silence lingered, and I knew I had to speak, I told them what Veruca had told me at the memorial.

"She was certain that Ian was having a fling with Esther. Does anyone remember her? She was an intern just before the second season."

The group shook their heads. Their faces were cast in night shadow and I felt the prick of judgment. I wondered if they were wondering why I remembered a summer intern from so long ago. I felt like I had tipped my hand.

"It must have been after Ian and I broke up again," Jasmine said. "I'm not surprised. Ian liked the ladies. At his age, he probably needed to recycle a few of us."

I was flush from the sidecar, from the wine, from the fresh memories of Ian. I felt claustrophobic, unable to share space with these other people. I got up and began taking in empty glasses from them, running them under water in the kitchen, hoping no one would spot the hot, salty tears that were stinging my eyes.

Perhaps sensing this, they left me alone. I could hear the faint sounds of their chatter, punctured by the occasional laugh. It occurred to me that Ian was a lot of things: a football fan with a private plane, a man with carnal appetites that included sex parties, a thoughtful co-worker who bought a gift that could express more than any of his words could. He was one person and many people. None of us had known the same man.

We lingered late into the evening. By midnight we had moved into the living room. Ford lit up another blunt. This time I took a drag. I had hit the point of drunkenness when I no longer cared much what I was doing.

"I meant to ask you all something," I said as I reached over into my handbag. I pulled out the business card that I had found in my car after the trip to Katonah. I passed it around and the group examined it.

"Have any of you ever seen this?" I asked.

"The image?" Jasmine asked, her words slurring slightly. She had drunk the most of all of us. "A lot of people in LA have this tattoo. I think it's a snake biting its own tail."

"Not the design. Have any of you received a card like this?"

All three shook their heads in unison.

"Where'd you get it?" Ford asked.

"It turned up in my car," I said. "I was in Westchester visiting a friend. I found it after I got back to the city. I guess it could have been slipped in at any point."

"Did you call the number?" Ford asked, turning the card over and then handing it to Corey.

I had gotten busy and hadn't tried it yet. I told them as much.

"It's strange," Corey said. "And kind of cool. I would call the number if I were you."

Jasmine got up and began cleaning the kitchen. Ford left the room in search of the bathroom.

"Hey, Maggie, I wanted to ask you a favor," Corey said when we were alone. "I've been staying here for the past few months, but with Jasmine back in town on a more permanent basis I feel like I should push on. My apartment in Morningside Heights is sublet until January 1st. Could I crash at your place for a few weeks?"

"No problem," I said. I had always liked Corey and spending time with him recently merely reinforced the feeling. Plus in the week since Peter had been gone, I hadn't yet adjusted to the empty apartment. I could use a distraction. "You have my number; just text me when you want to come over." We rose together from the couch.

As I was leaving the living room, I met Ford coming out of the bathroom.

"Want to share a cab?" I said. After tonight, I was feeling more comfortable with him. "I'm heading uptown."

"I'm fine on the subway," he said. "It's a straight shot to Ty's place."

Jasmine and Corey appeared in the hallway behind us, swiping kisses on our cheeks and promising to be in touch. Ford and I exited into the warm summer night. We walked along the street in companionable silence. As we got to the corner, I held my hand aloft to flag a cab.

"Listen, Maggie, there is something I wanted to tell you. I didn't want to say it in front of the others."

I dropped my arm and a taxi blared at me and then sped off. "What is it?"

"I got one of those business cards, too. I found it in my truck one day up in Ithaca."

"When?"

"A few weeks ago, maybe. And here's the thing: I called the number."

I was silent as I waited for him to say more.

"A woman answered. She said she wanted to talk with me. She was willing to come to Ithaca, so I met her for coffee."

"And?"

"And she was very professional. Nice person. She said she works for a man who hires actors for private parties. They pay good money for these gigs."

"Why all the secrecy?"

"She said her boss is very methodical. It's all part of creating the mood."

"So did anything come of it? Did they hire you?"

"No, but I thought about it. It was good money for an acting gig. She never contacted me again. I assumed it had fallen through."

I wondered why Ford had chosen to keep this private. What harm would have been done by telling Jasmine and Corey about it? A thought fleeted: was it possible only unemployed actors from the show were getting approached? In the years since *Wild Hearts* had ended, Jasmine and Corey had booked more work than Ford and I had. I batted the thought away.

"Well, this was fun," I said. "Are you free for dinner some time before you head back home? Maybe you and Ty?" I felt self-conscious, tacking on Ty's name to ease my nerves. I hadn't been single in years. I wasn't sure how to interact with men anymore.

"Possibly," he said. "Let's see how it plays out."

Ford gave me a salute as he ducked down into a subway stairwell. He was an oddball with a certain charm. I flagged down a taxi and jumped in. Cruising back towards my apartment, I felt a spark of happiness for the first time since I had heard about Ian's death. Spending time with the cast tonight had been like going back in time.

CHAPTER EIGHT
NOW

I WOKE TO the smell of bread wafting through my apartment. I rolled over happily. Corey appeared in the doorway, wearing blue jeans and a black t-shirt, holding a tray in his hand. "I couldn't sleep so I made myself useful," he said, setting it down on my lap. There was a slice of fresh black bread smeared with avocado paste and a mug of steaming black coffee. I took a sip gratefully.

Since Corey had arrived a few days before, we had been settling into a routine. He often woke me with a cup of coffee and the newspaper. Sometimes breakfast, too. I didn't want him to think of himself as the help, but he had taken to the role quite happily. I took a bite of toast. I could taste the sea salt and lime juice. "So with all this housesitting you do, Corey, are you ever tempted to snoop?"

He swatted my hand playfully. "You know it."

"Dish."

"Let's just say I've happened upon some strange things in basements." He arched his eyebrow playfully. "And once I've seen it, I can't unsee it."

"I need more info, Corey."

"I feel an obligation to protect your innocent mind."

"Can I ask you something else?" I said, taking another sip of coffee.

"Shoot," he replied.

"Twin brothers?"

He laughed. "I tell Jasmine all kinds of stories. I just like watching those pretty brown eyes grow wide."

"What time is it?" I said. I had no sense of life outside my window.

"The Showcase Showdown is on," Corey said, grabbing my remote and switching on my TV. It morphed into color and noise and the ersatz sounds of a studio audience. A contestant had spun the big wheel. *Forty, forty-five, you need that ten.* The host was saying. The audience gasped. *Oh, no. Fifteen gets you nowhere* he said.

After the episode was over, I took my toast and coffee and wandered into the living room. My apartment always looked different to me when I had guests. The ceilings seemed higher, the floorboards darker. It always took me time to adjust. Across the street, there was a church on the corner of Park and 90th. On Saturdays, I loved to sit with my breakfast and watch the wedding parties enter and exit. There had been hundreds over the years. I wondered how many of the couples were still together now.

"Corey, can I ask you something?" I said as he emerged from my kitchen with a mug of coffee.

"Of course," he said, dropping down and joining me on the couch.

"You said you saw Ian recently, right? At a party?"

"A few months ago, yes. It was not really my scene. A friend took me."

"Did you talk to him at all?"

"It wasn't really a talking party. What are you driving at?"

A theory had been forming in my mind since the memorial. This was the first time I was voicing it out loud. "Ian just didn't seem like the type to take his own life."

Corey considered this for a bit. "Depression can be insidious," he said. "I've had a few friends do it and I was shocked every time."

I let the comment hang in the air. Then I said, "But here's the thing. I think I may know someone who wanted to kill Ian."

Corey was puzzled. I realized I was being a bit provocative. "Do you remember Esther Oden, the intern?"

"You mentioned her the other night."

"She interned for us in the early days. It may have been before you were on the show, now that I think of it. At any rate, Ian and I did something terrible to her."

"We've all done terrible things, Maggie. Imagine if everyone with a vendetta acted on it. The world would have died out a long time ago."

"I ran into her recently. She seems to hate us still. And then Veruca told me something; that said she ran into them a few times together last summer. She was certain they were fucking."

"So Ian may have had a lover that the police didn't know about? Someone who harbored a grudge from a long time ago?"

"I don't know what the police know. I'm really just thinking out loud."

"I hear you, Maggie, but it's a bit implausible."

"Maybe."

"As I said, Maggie, we've all done horrible things. I doubt whatever you did to Esther was that bad. And if what Veruca said was true, it sounds like she and Ian had buried the hatchet."

"What terrible things have you done, Corey?" I felt a desire to be absolved by a comparatively worse revelation.

"Sadie Speed," he said. That sounded like a drag name.

"When I was in middle school, I was desperate to fit in. My mom and I lived on a houseboat and were dirt poor. She worked at the local diner. The rich kids in town used to go in and give her a hard time, order a bunch of food and then take off before she had served it. Fucked up shit like that. Anyway, a group of these clowns figured out I was her kid. They latched onto me. There was this girl at our school called Sadie Speed. She was sweet and smart but was never going to win any beauty pageants, if you catch my drift. The leader of the pack told her that I had a crush on her. It was an outright lie. No one knew I was gay but it's not like I dated girls ever. So the boys convinced me to write Sadie a note, telling her I wanted to meet her at the diner. Apparently she went crazy when she got it. She had always thought I was cute. And so on the day in question, the guys and I drove by the diner. We saw her sitting there, drinking her cherry Coke in a booth by the window. And then we drove to her house and covered the trees in her front yard with toilet paper."

"Jesus, Corey," I said, without masking my judgment. "That's awful."

"I know. I was a bastard. You feel better now?"

"That poor girl," I said. "What happened to her?"

"She was an outcast for the rest of the year, and then I left pretty soon after. But I ran into her years later at a Pride parade party in New Orleans with a guy I knew from our hometown. I wasn't sure if she recognized me, but she seemed happy."

I wondered if Riley had ever treated a girl like that. It turned my stomach to think about it. How could boys be so cruel?

"My point is that to this day I have never woken up to find Sadie Speed standing over my bed with a meat cleaver. I'd be pretty easy to find, too."

Corey had a point. I stood up, stretched, and took my plate and mug back to the kitchen.

"I am going to go run some errands," Corey said, coming in after me. "Do you need anything?"

I waved him off with a polite decline. When he was gone, I walked back into my bedroom and found my purse. There was something I had been meaning to do.

I found the business card, stuck in my wallet next to an old Metrocard, and pulled out my cell phone. There was an old, analog ring on the other line: six curt bleeps before a woman answered with a melodious greeting.

"I got your card," I said. "I found it in my car."

"And you'd like an appointment?"

"Yes, as soon as possible."

"I can meet with you tomorrow. I've got openings at 2:30 and 3."

I took the first slot and got directions from her to a bar in the West Village. It wasn't far from my old apartment on 13th street. It had been twenty years but I knew from memory the block the bar was on.

It was called The Eight Ball, something a passerby might glean from the wooden sign with a black pool ball that hung above it. It was on 7th Avenue near 12th Street. I arrived early, after it had opened but long before crowds of after-hours workers streamed in for craft ale and cocktails. The interior was red brick with black wooden floors. To my left as I entered, a woman was leaning over the countertop, slicing limes. An empty speed rail was on the counter. She didn't look up until I sat down on one of the barstools.

"Can I get you something?" she asked. She had long sheaths of black hair and gold rings on each finger.

"Club soda with a twist of lime," I said. "A lot of ice."

She nodded and went about fixing me my drink. After she served it, I slid down off my stool and wandered around the interior. There was a velvet curtain at the back, parted at the middle. I walked behind it to a smaller room with more intimate seating and a platform that could fit an earnest poet or a singer with an acoustic guitar. There were canvases on the wall, portraits of faces done in a slightly exaggerated fashion with bold colors and backdrops. I liked the aesthetic. One showed a little blonde girl with a hesitant smile, another was a middle-aged woman with John Lennon glasses and an elongated neck, and a third was bald man with dark eyelashes and gold hoop earrings. I snapped a picture of all three and of the artist's card that hung below.

"Aren't those great?" A woman said. She had slipped into the back room without my notice. She had long salon blonde hair, stylish eyewear, and a Burberry scarf. I could have easily mistaken her for any number of my Upper East Side neighbors. She was out of place in this bohemian setting. She looked like she summered in Hyannis and dated the sons of presidential candidates.

I took another sip of my drink: fizz and lime and chill.

"I used to come here in college," the woman said, walking over and taking a seat on a velvet couch. "That platform really takes me back. I fancied myself a folk singer in those days. I thought I had talent. That's the mark of an amateur, isn't it? Thinking you're better than you are?"

"Human nature, I suppose," I said in response. "The same reason we can't smell our own BO."

She focused her brown eyes on me as she gestured for me to take a seat opposite her. "So I'm sorry we had to be so cloak and dagger about this meeting," she said. "My boss is very particular about these things."

I was struck by how accurately Ford had described this woman. She had disarming warmth.

"I'm going to be straight with you, Ms. Grayson. My boss is crazy rich. He started an Internet company that went public five years ago and he sold it for a boatload. These days, he spends most of his time playing high-stakes poker and hosting parties."

"And this is where I come in? I'm the talent?"

"In a way, yes. Every once in a while, he hosts these private parties. He wants to please the clients, so he goes above and beyond. I don't know if you are aware of it, but *Wild Hearts* is very popular in certain foreign markets like Japan and Denmark. He is willing to pay big money."

"I have to make an appearance at these parties?"

"It's a little more complicated than that. And he insists on keeping the particulars private until you sign the contract. I can assure you that nothing illegal is going on. It will be the easiest money of your life."

I sat back, draining the last of my glass. I was somewhat intrigued by the proposal.

"I have to tell you, I am a fan of the show, too," she said. "I still watch it on YouTube. I think it's a little underrated gem. That whole plotline about Duncan in the attic reminds me of classic Hitchcock. And Mira and Jacoby just set my world on fire."

"Am I the only one you've approached?" I asked, still curious about this.

"It's strictly market-driven," she said. "My boss knows the actors who are popular and wants to please his clients. And if you're wondering, the people who come to these parties are the one percent. They have money to fly around the world for events like this."

Whatever had existed between Ian and me, it was now limited to our scenes in front of the camera. I felt a prick of wistful awareness that Ian and I would never interact again.

"Let me think about it," I said. I stood up from the velvet couch and walked back through the bar and onto the street. I was not in a frame of mind to be making any decisions.

CHAPTER NINE
NOW

By Labor Day, the heat had begun to break and with it, there was a feeling in the air of seasonal change. Riley and his roommate invited me over for brunch on the holiday. I selected a red dress and slipped it on over my head, pairing it with black flats. I grabbed a bottle of champagne to spice things up and carried it like a newborn down the elevator to the lobby and hailed a cab.

Riley was now less and less of a person and more of an abstraction, a collection of favorite moments over his eighteen years. I had an image I could never shake of him at two in his car seat, singing "Twinkle, Twinkle Little Star" as Peter drove us north to visit my mother. Riley couldn't make his r sounds so it always sounded like "Little Stah." At seven he was obsessed with astronomy. Peter and I bought out the REI camping section and slept under the stars with him in Connecticut. Two years later it was Pokémon that captivated him. I spent the night before Christmas that year hiding trading cards all over the apartment. He spent the next morning searching, always finding more.

Riley and Stefan lived in a fifth-floor walkup on Thompson Street in the village. There were black and white cracked tiles in the lobby, mailboxes that were broken open, and a wind shaft outside the windows that housed cooing gray pigeons. Peter and I had agreed earlier this summer that the extra rent was worth the experience in independence Riley would gain from living away from home. Still, I missed my son. I wasn't sure I would ever be able to let him go.

I could smell curry and fresh baking bread as I reached the top floor. The neighbor's television was blaring a Spanish telenovela. I hit the buzzer and knocked at the same time, not expecting much to work in a building like this.

"Just a sec," I heard behind the industrial brown door. There was a sound of locks turning before the door opened. Veronica, Riley's girlfriend, was standing there, wearing jean cutoffs with a brown tank top and a gold "V" on a chain around her neck. She was little over five feet with a round moon face and lion's mane of curly hair. She smelled of fresh linen and citrus shampoo.

"The boys are in the kitchen," she said, and I was instantly envious of her poise and casual confidence. "Do you want a tour?" She took the bottle from me, the paper bag crinkling as she walked me through a narrow corridor. I had been here once before, when we helped move Riley in. To the right as we walked, there were two bedrooms, a living room, bathroom, and then finally at the back a kitchen with large windows that opened to a rusting fire escape. I found my son by the stove, whisking melted butter, eggs, and flour together. His roommate was standing nearby, chopping a pineapple into chunks. On the eastern wall, there was a kitchen table with four chairs and mismatched place settings.

My son and I greeted each other while Veronica popped the cork and poured the bubbly in a glass pitcher. It was made of thin glass painted with roses, probably something they had picked up at a flea market, maybe old stock from a Mexican restaurant that had closed. She topped the fizz with pineapple juice and stirred.

"Mimosa?" She asked, offering me a glass Mason jar.

"Thank you," I said, making a mental note to sip slowly. Staying more sober than my son and his friends was essential.

Stefan was a gangly kid with ropey blond curls and a nose ring. Like many art students I had known, his body seemed to be a canvas for his message. He had tattoos in Sanskrit and kanji. He proffered a platter of pineapple slices and placed it in the center of the table.

My son was now pouring pancake batter into silver dollar size shapes onto a sizzling flat pan. My mother had taught him most of his cooking skills. When we visited her in Northampton, she would throw an apron around his neck and pull out a step stool so he could work at the counter beside her. She had taught him to make sourdough bread, cheese soufflé, even beignets.

The kids were bantering back and forth about a movie they had seen at the Angelika the night before. It sounded French and pretentious and horrible so I politely listened while they discussed the characters' motivation.

"You're an actress, tell us about it," Veronica said, turning her attention toward me across the table. "How do you embody a character?" She had big brown eyes and a smattering of freckles across her nose. It was no surprise to me that Riley had fallen for her. She was adorable.

"It's not hard," I said. "The character is an extension of you. I spent four years in college acting class honing my voice and facial control. The best advice I got was from my advisor. He said that you have to make every scene about the other actor. Work to make their scene good and yours will be better too."

"I've seen a few episodes on YouTube," Veronica said. "You're a really good crier."

I smiled appreciatively. It was true: I had a talent for calling up tears. I had a few carefully selected memories and movies scenes that could bring them up nearly every time. The problem was, if I got going too much I sometimes couldn't get the dialogue out. I had flubbed a few scenes because my voice was too choked up to be audible.

Riley moved over to the table with a platter of pancakes and vegetarian sausages. Soon the food was being passed around and we were bantering about all manner of topics: the latest exhibits at MOMA, the Republican candidate for president, whether America was really ready for a woman president. When Veronica reached over and took Riley's hand, I smiled without feeling it.

I was biting my last morsel when my phone pinged in my purse. I ignored it until the table was cleared. When Veronica shooed me away from cleanup, I went into the living room and fished it out of my handbag.

Without reading the screen, I hit the redial button.

"Maggie, thanks for returning my call so quickly." Cora, my agent, was on the other end of the line. She had a smoky hack of a voice that I could easily spot in an aural lineup. "Listen, I'm sorry to say that they hired another actress to play Pfeni."

My heart deflated. I exhaled.

"They liked you, they really did. I definitely think that I can get you another audition with this company next year. But they've got a lot to choose from, as you can imagine."

Next year. I had been through these cycles with Cora many times. Months would go by with me leaving cheerful messages – "*Cora, just checking in. I saw a performance at the Exit last night and it made me hungry to be back on the stage"* – Or another: "*Cora, just checking in. I know you'll be headed to Miami for the holidays so maybe we can talk before then?"*—With each passing one I was getting a little older, and a little less likely to be sent out for anything.

"You're such a good actress, Maggie. Have you seen the *Wild Hearts* comment boards on YouTube? Every year you're finding new fans."

"That's old work, Cora. I was in my twenties and thirties. Those roles are no longer an option for me."

"I know, doll. But I just need you to keep your spirits up. Take another acting class or get involved in a student film. Keep your skills fresh. Isn't your son at NYU? I bet the film school there could use some recognizable faces."

I had heard variations on this pep talk so many times. With each repetition it began to ring more and more hollow. I thanked her and hung up. I went back to the kitchen. The kids were debating the merits of junior year abroad. Stefan had done his in Florence and thought it was overrated.

"It's a town full of tourists," he opined, running a hand through his hair. "How is that authentic?"

"I think I need to shove off, kids," I said. "I know you've all got classes starting tomorrow so I don't want to keep you. Are you sure I can't do some of the washing up?"

They all simultaneously objected so I made the slow goodbye to the door. Riley walked me down the stairs.

"Mom, can I get you a Lyft?" he asked. I looked askance over my shoulder back at him. He knew how I felt about those companies. They were running yellow cabs out of business.

"How is your dad doing?" I asked him.

I hadn't talked to Peter since he moved out, just before Ian's memorial a few weeks ago.

"OK, I think," he replied, stepping outside with me into the breaking September heat. "It would be great if I could see the two of you together sometime."

I didn't love the idea but I would do anything for my son. "Let's have a family dinner in a few weeks," I said as the wheels to a yellow cab screeched to a halt in front of us. I swiped a kiss across his cheek as I jumped in. "Before the leaves turn."

I twisted around in my cracked vinyl seat as the car took off, watching as my son shrank in size on the sidewalk behind me. My eyes brimmed a bit, a mix of maternal love and champagne before noon.

I shook the image off, refocusing on my surroundings. My taxi driver was pontificating in some foreign language on his blue tooth. A newsreader on the radio was announcing the week's weather forecast. Outside around me, the village morphed into Midtown. Tourists walked by with shopping bags and sweaty bottles of pink lemonade. A hot dog vendor pushed his cart into the shade.

As we got nearer to home, I felt a chill dread at the thought of being alone in my apartment. Corey had gone to the Hamptons for the three-day weekend, but he would be back tomorrow.

I was hit by a wave of air-conditioned air and a waft of lilies as I entered the apartment. It was silent inside. I pulled off my dress and walked into the bathroom. We had a large bathtub and a separate steam shower, a choice of comforts, but instead I stood in front of the full-length mirror. My lower stomach was bulging slightly and I ran my hand over it. I had eaten and drunk a little too much today and I would pay for it tomorrow on the scale. I pushed two fingers together and stuck them down my throat, gagging until the food came up. I could taste pineapple and flour and spices.

I stepped into the shower and washed myself clean of the sweat and the sick and the city. I emerged into the bedroom wrapped in a towel with wet hair dripping down my naked shoulders. My bathrobe wasn't in its usual place. Across the street, a man in his apartment talked on his phone. I was half-naked in front of a window with a neighbor looking in my direction. I couldn't bring myself to care.

My phone dinged on my bed. I reached over and swiped up, expecting Page or Riley or maybe my mother. They were the only people I heard from regularly.

Instead there was a message from an unknown number. I hit replay.

"Maggie, hi, it's Catharine Nash calling you again. Happy Labor Day. Just wanted to let you know that my boss has a party coming up next weekend. It's going to be at building in the Meat Packing District. Strictly controlled guest list. I'd love to be able to get you on board. He's willing to pay $10,000 for four hours' work."

When the message ended, I hit replay. Catharine had such an inviting, pleasant voice. I wondered why she had given up on her musical aspirations. She was good-looking enough for show business. Maybe she just didn't feel a passion for it. What a blessing it must be not to be plagued by a yearning to perform.

I sat down on the bed, feeling the soft caress of the cotton towel around me. With the money she was offering me, I could rent a small theater for an evening and host a one-woman show. Maybe it would make a difference. Or maybe it would just feel good to be back on the stage.

I hit the redial button and waited for Catharine to pick up.

CHAPTER TEN
NOW

My bed was covered in colors: crimson, teal, azure. There were polka dots and stripes and small French poodles. Going through my closets on the day of the party, I had discovered that I owned twelve of Mira's swing dresses. I would need to wear one tonight.

Corey stood over the bed, discerning between them, trying to pick the right outfit for the return of Mira. "I would go for the black sheath," he said. "There is a reason it's a classic." He picked it up and placed the fabric up against his body. "Maybe jazz it up with some red pumps."

I ran my hand over my belly, aware of a protrusion. All the avocado toast and sashimi and vodka gimlets were showing up in my midsection. Even the occasional purge wasn't helping much.

"I like the black, but I think I'll go with the pink," I said, taking the frock from the bed and slipping into my bathroom. I shut the door and slipped off my string pants and t-shirt. I had spent the afternoon in one salon after another: my stylist had ironed my hair and then folded it into a tight chignon. My eyelashes were painted blue-black with vegetable dye. I'd gotten my nails polished, too.

I slipped the dress over my head and turned both ways in the full-length mirror. I applied lipstick and zipped up my side. As I stepped back out into the bedroom, Corey stood with his hand outstretched, holding the gold charm bracelet. He placed it on my arm, like a nervous suitor before prom, and shut the clasp.

"Am I crazy, Corey?" I asked, examining a row of pumps by the door before stepping into a pair of black ones. I was primped up, inches taller. "Some eccentric billionaire has a Mira fetish. Should I be feeding those impulses?"

"This is how Branson, Missouri began," Corey said. "There is a huge market for nostalgia. Just think of it as your reunion tour."

I liked the sound of that. Mira was being resurrected.

Corey walked me out through the foyer and into the lobby. I lifted his hand and kissed his fingers as I hit the elevator button. "You've got the pepper spray, right?" he said as the elevator doors opened and I stepped inside.

I was too nervous to laugh.

∞

The party was being held in an old industrial building in the Meat Packing district. I had a printout of instructions in my purse that I had reviewed a few times. I was to buzz the penthouse when I arrived and wait for further instructions.

When my taxi pulled up at the given address, it was still warm out. The sky was fading slowly from blue to black. Traffic streamed crosstown, horns blaring out as if in conversation with each other. Groups of perfumed girls in short dresses clicked down the cement in their stiletto heels, linking arms as they crossed intersections.

There was a set of white steps leading to a glass exterior. When I reached the top, I could see grey industrial carpet leading to a large silver elevator. There was an enormous Asian man in sunglasses sitting on a metal folding chair near the elevator doors.

I buzzed the penthouse button and waited. After a minute passed, I buzzed again. I glanced left and then right, a sideswipe of illuminated cityscape. After my third buzz, the beefy Asian guy stood up. He moved slowly, like a steamer moving through whitecaps, and opened the door. He grunted at me like a wrestler and turned around, leading me slowly to the elevator doors. After he hit the button and they opened, he stepped inside and pulled a chain from his pocket. He used a key to unlock access to the top floor. Then he illuminated the penthouse button and walked back to his folding chair.

The elevator ascended. When the doors parted on the top floor, I was in a cavernous open space. The floors were black and smooth as a dance floor. There were heavy beams crisscrossing the ceiling. The room was completely empty. I walked around, mesmerized by the views from the huge windows all around.

My heels clicked on the wooden floors. There was no one here. I began to feel some fear, wondering if I had just agreed to be locked inside a building for the night? I had my cell phone and could call the police if needed.

In the distance, as far from the elevator as you could walk, there was a platform. As I got nearer I saw that it was a set. I quickened my pace as the image came into view. The interior held a single bed with a bedpost, a full-length mirror, and a desk. There was a hairbrush and a looking glass on the desk, and a small stack of books on the nightstand near the bed. The closet was open and showed a rack of dresses. To the left, there were box windows and outside, a fake set of bushes.

It was unmistakable: this was Mira's bedroom. On the show, Mira had been hired by the Wilder family to nanny the younger children of the family patriarch. She lived in the servants' quarters with the family driver, Sam, and with Jacoby, who worked as a field hand in the vineyard. It was all very *Sabrina*, a movie that Julian loved and drew inspiration from when she created the story. In fact, most soap operas emulated classic movies. The large estates where multi-generational families lived were always modeled on Tara from *Gone with the Wind*, the manipulative gas lighting villains cribbed straight from noir. Nothing was ever new.

I stood for a few moments, drinking in the set and all the memories that went with it. Mira was an orphan who had grown up in foster care after her mother died. She and Sam developed a father-daughter bond that viewers loved. There were many scenes when he would stop into Mira's bedroom and they would have heart-to-hearts about Mira's growing love for bad boy Jacoby.

I stepped onto the bedroom floor. The books on the nightstand were journals. As I flipped through them, I saw that someone had painstakingly written out diary entries in a clear script.

"Amazing, isn't it?"

A voice from behind me cut the silence. I turned. "Do you feel like you're back there?"

I gasped, a bit nonplussed. It was Julian, dressed in her trademark rockabilly shirt and porkpie hat.

"You got an invite, too?" I asked her, at once startled and relieved to see a familiar face.

"Who do you think is writing the scripts?"

I hadn't until this moment considered that there might be a script. Of course they would need material for me to work from, but Catharine hadn't mentioned it.

"What do you know about this guy who hired us? My only contact has been with Catharine Nash."

Julian lifted an index finger and held it to her mouth, kissing it slightly, the international symbol for *shut the fuck up.*

In the distance the elevator dinged. A flurry of energy moved towards me. Veruca appeared, wearing a vibrant red Betsey Johnson dress. There were ruffles up and down the sleeves that brought to mind lasagna noodles.

"OK, I've got it," she said, handing Julian and me a thin script. It had a blue cover and about eight pages held together by a gold clasp. "We've got about an hour to rehearse. It should be enough time. The dialogue is minimal."

I opened to the first page, a call sheet. There was only one long scene, starting with the image of Mira admiring herself in the full-length mirror, unaware that Duncan was outside in the shrubbery surveilling her. Sam interrupted and the two had a discussion. Then, like all good soap scenes, it ended with a hook.

The elevator dinged again and soon the space was overwhelmed with caterers pushing food carts, setting up folding chairs, unpacking crates of booze. Apparently the party wouldn't begin for a while. A woman with a headset flurried around, barking orders at the set-up crew. They moved quickly, stringing hanging lights and bunches of multi-colored balloons, and covering the windows with white tulle curtains. An enchanting party atmosphere was forming, in stark contrast to the palpable stress in the air.

"So who's playing Sam and Duncan?" I asked. I hadn't talked to Ford since that night at Jasmine's. After our conversation that night I wasn't expecting him to reprise the role.

Julian and Veruca shrugged in unison. They didn't seem to know much more than I did. I took a seat on Mira's bed and began to page through the script. I didn't have much dialogue. In fact, I had done scenes like this so many times that this would be a breeze. I dropped the script and picked up one of Mira's diaries.

Someone had gone through and created journal entries. They were dated September and October 1996, which corresponded with the first few months of the series. They were in Mira's voice.

> *September 18, 1996*
> *Last night was the vineyard crush. Jacoby pulled me up into a barrel and I squished the grapes with my naked toes. They felt like wet sand oozing. The Wilders opened bottle after bottle of last year's vintage and I drank until my teeth were as stained as my feet. Jacoby was incredibly kind to me. At the end of the crush, he pulled over a bucket of soapy water and washed my feet. I felt like a princess being bathed before a ball. I can still feel his strong hands on me, serving me without a hint of roughness.*
> *October 3, 1996*
> *Jacoby stopped by last night and we talked until I fell asleep. His mother died when he was thirteen. Why didn't I know that? It felt so good to be talking to someone who just gets me, gets it. For so long, I have had a hole in my heart, but the more I talk to him, the more I feel like it can be healed. Maybe our mothers are looking down on us now, thrilled to have been a part of this.*

I continued paging through the entries. Whoever had written them had a good sense of Mira's internal voice. They went on for some time, mentioning the menacing fear she felt when she was home alone at night. They also got more explicit in her attraction to Jacoby.

Towards the end of the journal, the pages went blank. I flipped through them, watching the white flutter past. As I did, my attention was captured by some ink towards the end. I opened to a page near the back. In a different pen color, someone had scrawled a note. The writing was sloppy, as if written quickly and without much care. I read it and then read it again. A gasp escaped my lips.

> *Mira, if you can read this, it's Jacoby. I need your help. They're going to poison the vintage.*

CHAPTER ELEVEN
NOW

I HELD THE diary in my hand, not quite comprehending what I was seeing. I couldn't remember what Ian's handwriting looked like. We had sat side-by-side at many fan luncheons, scribbling our names in black Sharpie onto 8-by-10 glossies before handing them over to the housewives and college undergrads that had waited in long lines to meet us. *Love and Light, Maggie. All My Love, Ian.* I imagined him signing his name in a loopy, unrestrained script. It was a created memory, though, something I pieced together sitting here on the set.

The room was beginning to empty out from the party set-up. There was a distinct shift from frenzied busyness to the prepared stillness before guests arrive.

I pulled my phone out of my handbag and surreptitiously took a snap of the page.

Lara Stone had arrived, wearing huge eyeglasses and a black silk shirt that nicely offset her auburn curls. She was an attractive woman, briefly an actress, who had been our set designer for many years.

"Is this your work?" I said, gesturing behind me to Mira's bedroom. "It's an exact replica."

"I had to do it pretty much from memory," she said, leaning over to swipe a kiss across my cheek. "So thank you."

I hadn't seen Lara in years but had always liked her. She dispelled the cliché that show business was full of phony people. She had an earnest sensibility that I had always trusted.

The elevator doors rolled open and a man swished over. He was dressed in a tailored black jacket and bowtie. "Such a pleasure to meet you," he said, bowing slightly to me. He was a Nordic blond who spoke with a mild accent. "I'm Sebastian Detlefsen." Catharine Nash was just behind him, holding a stack of papers in her hand. Her hair was pulled up into a chignon and she was run some gloss over her lips.

"Alright, so I need the talent to come with me," she said, gesturing to an area behind the set. I followed her to a heavy black door, which she unlocked and swung open. The room was largely empty save for a few dressing curtains and a nearly empty rolling clothing rack. There were a few tackle boxes open on a table near a sink.

"You can just sit here and run lines by yourself," she said. "I'm waiting on two others who are running late."

She left in a flurry and I was now alone, script in hand. I pulled out my phone and sent a text. A few moments later Veruca appeared.

"You rang?" she said, taking a seat next to me on a folding chair.

"You said you saw Ian and Esther together a few months ago, right?"

"Did I?" she said, examining the paint on her nails. She was holding a flute of pink champagne.

"Yes, after Ian's memorial you said you had seen them together on Long Island over the summer."

"Oh, right," she said. "Yes, I saw them a few times at Dottie's having breakfast. She had that sweaty glowy sex vibe. I'm certain they were fucking."

Aiming to pierce my heart, Veruca had succeeded.

"Can you tell me anything else about it?"

"You're not going to go all Miss Marple on us, are you? Stanch your grief by creating some outlandish theory about how Ian died?"

My cheeks burned. This woman could see right through me.

"What I can tell you I think I already have. I ran into Ian and Esther a few times over the summer. But I'm not surprised Ian killed himself. He always had demons."

"What do you mean?" I asked.

"Ian used to come and find me at the studio on his breaks. We went to the roof and smoked weed all the time. He was a tortured guy. His mother abandoned him when he was nine to take off to some feminist cult. He was very fucked up about it."

This was more detail than Ian had ever given me. He had told me about that day in the garden, when he last saw his mother. She had abandoned the family when Ian was nine and his sister seven. But that was all I knew.

"And he had this weird thing," she said, taking a sip of champagne. Her lipstick left a noticeable smudge on the glass. "He said that Tamberlain communicated to him telepathically. He could hear her voice in his head, telling him that his mother was OK."

The door swung open and Catharine appeared with two men. They were a study in contrasts: one was a hunky dreamboat and the other had leathery skin and a stooped back.

"Maggie, I would like to introduce you to Hunter and David, who will be playing Sam and Duncan tonight." They both walked over and we shook hands. "You've got about forty minutes to run lines. I'll be back when we're ready for you."

She disappeared again. Veruca got up from her seat and walked toward the exit. "Can I get you anything? There's an open bar," she said to the three of us.

The men requested mineral water. I declined. We took our seats in a circle of folding chairs and began to review the script. Mira was already flooding back to me: her earnest sincerity and dreamy optimism.

When we had run the scene twice, I reached over for my phone and tapped in a text.

Who is Tamberlain?

A few minutes later it buzzed.

The leader of this cult his mom joined.

I wasn't sure how much I could trust Veruca's stories. I don't think she was outright lying, but I also wasn't sure of how accurate her interpretations were.

I typed another text: *do you remember where the cult was?*

A pause, then a ping.

Upstate, I think. Maybe Syracuse.

I thought back to that ethnography I had purchased at the Ithaca College bookstore. I had paged through it a bit when I got back to the city without reading it too closely. It was a series of first-person narratives from the residents of a place called Concordia. Could this be the feminist cult that Ian's mother had run off to? One thing was certain: I would read up on it when I got home.

Catharine appeared again, urging us to get in line by the door. David and I were on first. Mira would be alone in her bedroom, assessing herself in a full-length mirror, unaware that Duncan was standing outside her window. He was costumed in a turquoise silk scarf, Jackie O glasses, and a black women's wig.

We padded out soundlessly, entering the set from an obscured area behind. When I stepped on the floorboards, I could sense a small crowd of people standing at a distance, watching me. I moved around Mira's bedroom, running the brush through my hair. I wandered over to the bed and paged through the journals.

Outside the window, Duncan lurked. I could sense tension in the audience as I got up from her bed and moved near the window, as Mira was unaware of the danger that was outside. I could see him, of course, but I had to act like I couldn't. There was a shuffle of feet on the floorboards, a mild cough.

"There you are. Didn't you hear me calling your name?" Hunter-as-Sam was standing in the doorway. He didn't look much like the original actor, but he had the right build to embody the character. He entered and we sat together, talking on Mira's bed. Sam was meant to be a father figure to Mira, the orphan, and also the gentle matchmaker for her and Jacoby. In this scene, they talked mostly about him.

After the exchange, Hunter-As-Sam got up and said, "I'm going over to Avalon. Valentina is auditioning bands tonight. Wanna come?"

Valentina and Mira were rivals on the show. She was the daughter of the central family, a music producer who also owned the local nightclub. "I think Valentina would rather put a lit cigarette out in her arm than socialize with me," I said.

Hunter-As-Sam shook his head and chuckled softly. "Have it your way," he said as he got up and moved to the door. "Be sure to lock the door before you go to bed."

There was a mild gasp in the audience as they realized that Mira was now alone in the unlocked guesthouse with Duncan outside the window. After a beat, Mira went back to the full-length mirror, dropping her swing dress to the floor. She was dressed in black lingerie underneath. She pivoted back and forth, admiring herself in the mirror, and then caught a glimpse of something. When she turned to the window, she saw Duncan and screamed.

The crowd made a polite round of applause as the lights came up. I turned and gave a cursory bow, then waited for David and Hunter to join me. We clasped hands and bowed together. From the back of the room near the elevator, music blared through speakers. Cheap Trick's "Surrender."

Veruca appeared onstage with three champagne flutes; we all took one this time. I slipped back into the changing room to pull my dress back on. David stripped out of his Duncan costume and dropped the wig, sunglasses, and turquoise headscarf near the tackle boxes. We rejoined the crowd and lingered a bit with them, a group of about thirty Asian women. Like most fans I had met in my life, they were all very kind.

"I thought of something else," Veruca said as she sauntered over to me near the end of the evening. "I got curious once about Ian's mother so I Googled her. She is in prison."

"Do you remember her name?" I asked.

"Hannah," Veruca said. "No wait, Johanna. She had a different last name from Ian. Something short."

I was getting more and more information that I wanted to follow up on. First I needed to do my final circle, thanking fans for coming and saying goodbye to those I knew.

As I exited the building and hailed a cab, I couldn't deny that Catharine had been right. This had been the easiest money of my life. It was gratifying to be on set again, too. I was glad I had done it. And now I had some research to do.

When I got home, I went straight to Riley's room, hoping to find Corey there. There were signs of him everywhere: a stack of pressed and folded t-shirts, a laptop open to a music streaming service, a half-empty glass of water. A sweep of the apartment proved that I was alone. Since he had been staying with me, he often disappeared at night, not showing up until dawn. I couldn't imagine the life of adventure he led. I felt boring in comparison.

I went to my bedroom. In a room off the master suite, Peter had an office. When he moved out, he had left his desktop computer and a shelf full of books but had otherwise cleared out any remnants of him. I found the ethnography where I had left it: wedged amidst Peter's espionage thrillers and historical biographies. He was a particular fan of David McCullough and had left behind an autographed copy of *1776* that I had given him one Christmas. I wondered if that was a signal of some kind.

I paged through the ethnography, taking it back to my bedroom to read. There was a plate full of photographs in the center of the edition: images of the chapel, schoolroom, and fields at Concordia. There was one picture of a group of about thirty adults and children standing in front of two-story structure. After an introduction written by the author, there were individual sections centered around a theme. Each section had different chapters narrated by former residents. I flipped open to one in the section titled *Closure.*

> *It's easy to talk about the early days at Concordia but hard to talk about the end. My children were born there, on late winter evenings, with the midwives moving in and out of my cabin to stoke the fire or give me ice chips. My children would have been different people if I hadn't birthed them at Concordia. The night air, the apple blossoms, the rushing creek water entered into their souls when they took their first breaths. We had to walk away and my heart felt that loss for a long time.*

I shut the book. Could this have been the place that Ian's mother lived? I paged though a bit more, women's names flapping by with the pages: *Carlisle, Isidora, Lorenza.* I settled on one written by a woman named Tamberlain. It was in the section titled *Faith.*

> *From the hills we came, the only sound our naked feet raising the dust.*

We were one line, a serpent, moving towards salvation. The limbs were heavy with fruit, enlightened like our wombs, as we moved towards stardust.

I closed the book and fished my phone out of my purse. I scanned my texts until I found the one I had sent to Veruca earlier.

Who is Tamberlain? I had typed.

Veruca's reply came a few minutes later: *The leader of this cult his mother joined.*

I pulled up the photo I had taken of the journal page. *Mira, if you can read this, it's Jacoby. I need your help. They're going to poison the vintage.*

I wasn't sure what any of this meant, but I knew what I had to do. I lifted my phone again, sent a text, and went to the closet to pack a suitcase. I planned to be gone for a few days.

CHAPTER TWELVE
NOW

The bookstore was called Venus Envy. It was on the main commercial strip in Ithaca between a bakery and a hardware store. It was the third independent bookstore I had hit that day and the last one left. This had to be the shop owned by Esther Oden and her ex-boyfriend. From the Google searching I had done, I think his name was Rustin Wallace.

A bell rang as I entered but I didn't see anyone inside. There were long rows of wooden bookshelves painted in sequential rainbow colors and a kid's play area in the back. I browsed the travel section, paging through a Frommer's *Guide to New Orleans*. Trees dripping with Spanish moss and Garden District houses were transporting me when I heard someone emerge from a back room. He was about six feet with short dreadlocks. His boots clomped as he passed me.

"I was about to put in the order for sandwiches," he said to me as he moved past. "The special today is pesto nutloaf."

I smiled politely, pretending I knew what he meant. "I can't stay long," I said.

"Oh, I thought you were here for the book club," he said, sticking a key into the register and turning it. The machine began to chuff out a long paper receipt. "We're discussing *The Girl on the Train.*"

I had read that book in Italy and didn't much care for it. Still, it meant I could fake my way through a conversation if it came to that.

"You an out-of-towner?" He asked, taking out a pair of eyeglasses and putting them on his nose. He squinted at a number on the receipt. "Don't know that I've seen you before."

"I'm just passing through on my way to Northampton," I said. It was true, which helped; my mother was making my favorite casserole for dinner and expected me by six-thirty.

"Can I help you find something?" he asked, coming out from behind the front register.

"Maybe a book or two to read while I'm at my mother's," I said.

"Tell me some of your favorite titles, I'll give you a recommendation."

This was a bit of a stumper. I often abandoned books half-finished. "*The Wind-Up Bird Chronicle,*" I said. I had devoured it when I was pregnant with Riley. "And I loved *Geek Love.*" That was really dating me. I had read it my first year out of Barnard.

"Good taste," he said, swishing past me. He pulled a few titles from the fiction row. "*The Goldfinch* won the Pulitzer last year," he said, handing me a thick tome. "I can't find anyone who didn't like it. And the best book I've read recently was *All The Light You Cannot See.*" I took both books in hand and grabbed the guide to New Orleans as well. I felt an obligation to support his business.

As he rang up my purchases, the bell above the door rang and a trio of women entered. He greeted them over my head, "You all in for lunch, ladies? Pesto nutloaf?"

They murmured assent. One of them, in jean overalls and pigtails, hoisted a pink box aloft. "I brought dessert."

"Such a nice tradition, a book group," I said banally.

"Every second Sunday at one," he said.

I took my purchases and left the store, casting a furtive glance back inside to the women in the book club. They were standing in a gaggle chatting, oblivious to my presence. Once on the street, I walked quickly and turned the corner. I had parked my car on a side street, out of direct view. I climbed in, turned the engine, and entered an address into the GPS. I expected it would take about fifteen minutes to get there.

ꟹ

After I had driven for a while on the highway, the GPS directed me to an exit that led to a rural route. There were a few houses nestled in the hills, mailboxes at the end of their drives the main sign of life. After I passed under a covered bridge, the road began to steepen. A copse of trees lined the slope upwards. At the designated spot, I pulled off onto a dirt road and drove for a half-mile. In front of me in the distance was a small wooden village. There was a creek running beside it and in the distance an apple orchard. There were ten identical A-frame houses on either side of a grassy path, a chapel on a hill, and a larger building that I recognized from a photograph in the book.

I parked near the creek bank and got out. Below me, the ropey current churned. It was quiet save for the twitter of birdsong in the distance. A wind picked up as I walked closer to the line of houses.

I turned the porcelain door handle to one of the A frames. It was unlocked. Inside, there were thick floorboards, a potbellied stove in the middle of the room, and a small sink in back. There was a wooden ladder leading to a loft. I tried to imagine a cold winter in this place. It brought a whole new layer to the term cabin fever.

I continued walking down the path the lined the houses and moved up a sharp incline to an apple orchard. There was a cluster of trees heavy with low-hanging fruit.

Behind the orchard on the peak of a hill was a chapel. I scaled the incline and pushed open the oak door. Inside there were wooden pews and a small stone altar at the front. Above the altar there was a stained glass window. In it, a woman with long, copper-colored hair was standing naked with a plump apple in her hand.

I had read that this group worshipped Eve. They took communion every Sunday on a sliced apple. It was meant to be a symbolic reversal of the fall. Women had been blamed for the downfall of humanity and the liturgy challenged that. Wisdom and knowledge were something to be celebrated, not punished. I thought of the painting I had bought on the day I visited Esther at Ithaca College. I wondered if orchards in this area had inspired the artist.

"My husband called this the titty chapel," a voice said behind me. I turned and saw an elderly woman in a flowered top and loose skirt. She was wearing study hiking boots and holding a set of hedge clippers in one hand. In the other, she had a posey of apple blossoms.

"Sorry, I guess I'm trespassing," I said. "I read about this place and was curious."

"No worries," she said. "I promised the current owner I would look out for this place. He lives in Maine now."

"It's such beautiful land. I can't imagine giving it up."

"Oh, it wasn't their choice, believe me. The FBI shut them down."

This was news to me. While the book made oblique references to a closure, there were no specific details.

"Why did the FBI raid this place?" I asked her. The land was so peaceful. It was hard to believe anything bad could happen here.

"A young boy died," she said. "Right over there in that creek. He drowned. After it happened, his mother went to the Feds. Apparently there were all kinds of illegal things happening here. Marijuana cultivation, child abuse. A few people got sent up."

"And those that didn't? Any idea where they went?"

"Some moved into town, others moved away. There is a bookstore in town owned by a man who grew up here. Rustin Wallace is his name."

I had just met him. And if I could believe what Veruca had told me, he had a teenage son with Esther.

"I can show you the school, too, if you're curious." She said. "They did everything here. It was a community unto itself."

I nodded assent and followed her out. The earth was uneven walking down the hill so we moved slowly, as if on slippery rocks. When we got to the footpath near the A frames, it leveled out.

"How many residents were there?"

"I think it varied. Their leader was a woman named Tamberlain. She was a seminary dropout from the Bay Area. She moved here with her kids and some of her friends. Then other families joined them. They used to have a booth at the farmers' market. Someone here made exceptional sour dough bread. I always bought a loaf or two. Incredible blackberry jam in season, too."

"And your husband? What did he think of it?"

She chuckled slightly as we went up another incline to a structure that was above the A-frames. "Oh, Gus was a bit intimidated by the girl power factor. He had some pretty rigid beliefs. He always liked that bread and jam, though."

We had reached a large oak door. She pulled out a ring of keys, sorted through them, and stuck a gold one into the lock. It resisted a bit so I reached over and helped her jimmy it open. Her hands were rough with age.

"My name is Gretel Stevens, by the way," she said as she swung open the door. "My mother was a big *Sound of Music* fan. My siblings are Marta and Kurt."

"I love that movie," I said. My mother and I had watched it every Easter when I was growing up.

We entered into a dark, musty hallway that had large rooms on either side. On the left there was a traditional schoolroom and on the right a kitchen. I glanced around, imagining small groups of children working on craft and cooking projects.

"There was a library, too," Gretel said, leading me up a wide set of stairs to a stately room with built-in bookcases.

"It seems like a great environment for children," I said. "Hard to believe there was any trouble. You mentioned their leader, Tamberlain. Any idea what happened to her?"

"She was one of the ones who got sent away. I think she did five years at Finger Lakes Correctional. But I've seen her around town since then. She's hard to miss. Huge Afro. She wears these maxi dresses and bracelets up and down her arms. She co-owns that bookstore with her son."

So Esther's baby daddy was the son of the woman in charge of Concordia. She may have had some connections here, too.

"I really appreciate the tour," I told Gretel. "I'm lucky I ran into you."

As we parted, she handed me a posy of apple blossoms. "Flowers for my queen," she said. "I can't tell you how much Gus and I enjoyed *Wild Hearts.*"

As I hit western Mass, I began to feel connected again to my childhood. The highways and road signs as I neared Northampton were as familiar to me as family members. When I saw my first Friendly's sign, it made me ache a bit. Mom and I had gone there every Friday when I was a kid. We always split a cheeseburger and an M&M sundae.

I took Exit 19 towards King Street. When I reached Summer Street, I pulled up to a gray house with a wraparound porch. I felt my childhood crowding around me as I got out of my car. There was a gust of wind, hinting at autumn. It had cooled down since I drove north. It was starting to feel like the fall.

Up on the porch, the front door swung open and with it, I felt the thrill of reunion. I fell into my mom's soft arms and, over her shoulder, looked into the house where I had grown up. David, her boyfriend, was sitting in my favorite green chair. The TV was on with the volume muted. The walls were lined with white bookshelves. My mother had made tableau in most of them, with framed photographs, books, and memorabilia from different stages of our lives. Each one was like seeing a season of the past.

"I've made your favorite meal," my mom said. "And corn bread. It should be ready in about fifteen minutes."

I walked over to where David was now standing. He had brown hair and glasses and soft bulging cheeks that reminded me of a baby. I took his frail body in mine. After being single for most of my childhood, Mom had met David ten years before when she stopped by his dealership hoping to trade in her Dodge Dart for a Honda Civic. He made her a generous offer and she invited him over for dinner. They had never married but they were as solid a couple as I knew.

"We've just been watching the news," Mom said, switching the muted set off. "Horrible story in Holyoke. A vagrant walked into the supermarket and stabbed a clerk. Just took a swipe at her neck with a serrated knife."

Northampton and the surrounding area had had a problem with homeless people since the 1980s. A state-run mental health hospital had closed due to budget cuts, displacing over a thousand residents. Many still roamed the streets, asking for change and sleeping in the park near the Peter Pan bus station.

"How awful. Is the clerk going to survive?" I asked.

"She's at Northampton General, in surgery. Serious condition. Mother of a four-year-old, apparently."

I cast a glance into the kitchen, where Mom had set the table.

"You expecting company?" I asked, noting the four place settings. Before she could answer, there was a steady knock at front door. My mouth gaped open a bit when I saw the hulking body of Ty Harris, my former co-star, filling the front hall of my childhood home.

"Look who I ran into outside of Gillette," Mom said. "I invited him for dinner."

I mouthed surprise and leaned up to embrace Ty. I hadn't talked to him since Ian's memorial.

"You two ran into each other?" I said. "That's bananas."

"I am up helping Marley move," Ty said. "She didn't like her house in the quad and went in a lottery to get a new slot. She's now in Northup."

"Northrup," Mom corrected. She had worked in dining services just across from Northrup for many years. On weekends, she cooked for both houses.

"What was it like growing up in the shadow of this school?" Ty said as we took a seat in the front room. Mom took drink orders: cranberry juice, water, club soda. "Townies must resent the hell out of the students."

"It's complicated," I said. "The school has employed many locals for years. And they helped me get into Barnard."

"Marley doesn't love it here. She has talked about transferring. She said it's just intensely competitive. But I hope she'll hold out and Asher will join her up here. I toured Williston Northampton yesterday. I'm hoping he'll do his last year of high school there."

Mom returned with four lowballs, drinks and ice and disks of lime, and we all clinked glasses.

"So this is where you grew up, huh?" Ty said, raking a glance around the living room and out to the front porch. An elderly couple walked by with a small dog on a leash.

"We moved in when she was three," Mom said. "For years the landlord rented out the basement apartment to students." When I landed the role of Mira and a three-year contract, I bought the house for mom. The housing market in the area made it difficult for certain people to own homes. Even professors at the school sometimes lived in apartments.

"We had some great neighbors," I said. "Remember Oscar?"

Oscar had lived with us for five years starting when I was in middle school. He was doing a PhD at U Mass in political science. At the time, Oscar was living as a woman named Christa. She was from Switzerland, and liked to use our kitchen to bake braided bread. When he turned up years later to visit, after the gender reassignment surgery, we were in for a bit of a shock.

"Dinner's almost ready," Mom said. We got up and walked slowly back to the kitchen.

There was a heavy blue ceramic serving dish in the center of the table and a wicker basket full of corn muffins near a covered butter dish. Mom brought over a glass pitcher of ice water.

"We have been watching old episodes of the show on YouTube," Mom said, as she took a seat with us. "David loves it."

"My mom used to love soaps," he said. "I grew up watching them. I love that whole Duncan character. And the vineyard setting."

"I didn't realize we were up on YouTube," Ty said. "Might be fun to see some old episodes."

"We just saw the one where Jacoby steals Mira away from her wedding to Joshua. So romantic." My mom said, splitting a corn bread muffin into two and slathering butter on it.

I remembered that day. We had filmed on location at a Quaker church in Connecticut. Beneath my antique lace dress, I was newly pregnant with Riley. In a few months on the show, Mira would begin to feel sick. She gave birth to Sandrine a few months after I came back from maternity leave.

"Joshua just never stood a chance," Ty said. "No one wanted him with Mira. I hated being the stooge in that plot."

He was right, in a way. Joshua was a supporting character whose main purpose was to get in the way of true love. It must have been frustrating to play the role. I was lucky that Mira got better plotlines.

"And yet we did get married," I said, taking a bite of the casserole. It was shredded chicken, bowtie pasta, and a delectable herb sauce. "Mira went back to Joshua when she discovered Jacoby had been in prison for killing his stepfather."

"Spoiler alert," Ty said, raking a hand through his thick black hair.

"What have you been doing since the show ended?" David asked.

"This and that," Ty said evasively. I had seen him in a guest shot on a NY-based sitcom playing a man who howled like a wolf when he had an orgasm. I was guessing he didn't want to advertise it. "I just filmed a coffee commercial in London."

We continued eating and chatting as the sun began to set over the backyard.

"It's just shocking news about your co-star," Mom said. "I would think someone like that would have everything to live for."

"He had his demons," I said. "His mother abandoned him when he was nine."

"Oh my stars," she said. "I think there's a special place in hell for women who do that."

I understood her judgment, in a way. She had done the hard to work to raise me for eighteen years. And yet the fact that Ian's mother was incarcerated made me wonder if there might be more to the story. Maybe Ian was better off without her.

"I can't understand it either," Ty said. "My son is living in Chicago this year with his mother. I miss him so much. How can someone be so cold to their own flesh and blood?"

My mother scrutinized him with an inscrutable expression. I couldn't tell if she was judging his domestic situation or wondering where her life would have gone if she'd had a father for me.

We finished up dinner, stacking up our dishes in the sink. Mom offered to make coffee and Ty gratefully accepted. He had a long drive ahead of him back to the city.

We lingered in the TV room for a bit, sipping coffee and eating Bordeaux cookies. When the sun began to go down, Ty thanked my mother for dinner and got up.

"I guess I'll see you again sometime. I hope anyway," Ty said, reaching over to give me a hug after we got congregated outside on the front lawn. "Don't be a stranger." David, Mom, and I stood by as he drove off. He tapped the horn lightly as he turned onto King Street.

"He must be lonely," Mom said. "Coming all the way up here to help his daughter move?"

"I think he's just a good parent," I said, more coldly than I intended. I saw my mother flinch: the unspoken tension of an imperfect relationship. When I had left for college, she had bought me a Peter Pan bus ticket and packed me a lunch. I remember the sting of arriving at my dorm and watching parents decorating their daughters' rooms. I think my mother saw parenting as an eighteen-year obligation like a mortgage. When I left home, she earned her blessed freedom. She rarely contacted me during my first years in New York, but after I had Riley I had insisted on a weekly Sunday call. If I hadn't been consistent with it, I probably would have heard from her only a few times a year.

I grabbed my overnight bag from the hallway and barreled up the stairs to my old bedroom. Years ago, Mom and I had put up the blue flowered wallpaper. I had hung a Rick Springfield poster over my bed. Near my window there was a bookshelf full of paperback Harlequin romances and a stack of vinyl on the floor: Peter Gabriel, Madonna, Michael Jackson. It was my childhood frozen in time. Thinking back to the girl I was then, I never could have foreseen what coming next: the success on the show, the affair with Ian, the slow decline into the ennui of middle age. The blissful canopy of teenage ignorance had protected me from what was coming next. I never would have imagined, back then, that I was capable of doing bad things. I thought I was a good person. Wasn't everyone?

It occurred to me now that I had been more similar to Esther than I had wanted to acknowledge. Maybe that was why I took an instant dislike to her when I met her that day at Absinthe, and why I was so competitive with her about Ian. He didn't see much difference between us. And in that realization, I knew how easily either one of us could have been replaced.

CHAPTER THIRTEEN
THEN

ON THE FIRST night of the shadow game, Ian took me out for oysters near the sound. They were served in front of us in a long glass dish filled with ice chips. Ian slurped them down between sips of Jack Daniels. I had a handcrafted cocktail, a bad match for the oysters, but I drank it anyway to burn off my nerves. I didn't want to do this. I didn't like the oysters either but I ate a few just to ease the hunger. They were smoky and slimy and disgusting.

When we got home, we moved through his quiet house back to his bedroom. His bed was elevated and beneath a skylight. He lifted me to the edge of the bed and lay me back, peeling off my panties slowly. He dropped them to the floor and buried his tongue into me, licking my labia and then finding my clit. I arched my back, enjoying the sensation, but I kept an eye on the closet door.

When he was finished, Ian lifted me back up. He pants were undone now and his erect cock stood to attention. I leaned over and licked the head, never one to go too deep, and listened to him moan. He pushed me back and entered me, fucking me. There was a slight feeling of pain with the pleasure. I kept my eye on the closet door but it didn't move. When he yelped slightly and fell onto me, I knew the first night was over.

Esther was not there.

On the second night, Ian took me for sushi. We ordered an enormous platter and I ate with gusto, dipping nigiri and California rolls into soy sauce. We had sake too, warm and acidic, and by the time we got home we were falling over each other. Ian pulled me onto the couch, his pants unzipped, but I steered him back to his room, wanting to observe the rules. He kissed me deeply, tenderly, and I wanted to stay like that, me on the edge of his enormous bed, my legs wrapped around his torso. I didn't want an intrusion, a watcher, a surprise.

Ian slowly stripped my dress and panties off and I did the same with his black jeans and t-shirt. Soon we were bare and I was on top of him, moving rhythmically to the quiet of the cottage. Ian was smiling devilishly now, inhaling before he came hard.

I felt a soft set of nipples behind me, pressing lightly into my back, and I was aware now that we weren't alone, that while Ian and I were fucking, the closet door had opened and Esther was there, naked, standing behind me.

Ian sat up, pushing me aside, and soon he was licking Esther's nipples. She threw her head back, breathing deeply. I moved my legs around Ian, his back facing me, and now we were on either side of him. He was sucking Esther's breasts while I pressed mine into him.

He pushed me back and now he was fucking Esther full on, Ian on the edge of the bed and Esther standing near him. I could see her face in silhouette contorted in a pleasure that made me wince with anger, with jealousy. I moved back like a child who had been wounded, hating the moment. As I watched Ian and Esther together, I felt a shudder of revulsion.

Later, when I was alone, removed from both of them, I could not shake the feeling of betrayal. Ian had loved Esther's fat, bulbous body. He had loved her gigantic breasts. How foolish had I been to think that Ian wouldn't find her attractive? In that moment, I knew something I couldn't forget: Ian was attracted to all women. Past a certain point, and I had seen it tonight, he was not aesthetic. There was no difference between Esther and me.

Maybe, I thought, this was where monogamy had originated: in a moment like this of pure carnality where lawlessness brings chaos. Sexuality was an appetite that needed to be controlled, just as surely as people needed food rules and speed limits.

I had made a mistake in letting Ian talk me into this. Repulsed by our encounter with Esther, I was ready to be an ascetic. Ian was like a toddler eating sugar for breakfast. We were doomed.

But before I could accept any of this, I knew I had to get rid of Esther Oden. I could not see her face again, or contemplate us as equals. I went to Julian the next week and used my star power to get her fired. I don't know what they told her, but she was gone the next time I dropped in the writers' office. Her night with Ian and me had cost her. I never saw or heard from her again.

CHAPTER FOURTEEN
NOW

WHEN I GOT back from Northampton, I settled back into a strict routine. It was the easiest way for me to keep my loneliness at bay. Riley was busy with his first semester at NYU. I hadn't spent time with him since Labor Day. My mother and I had a standing Sunday call although it never went longer than ten minutes. And Corey was still staying with me although I didn't see him as often as I would have liked. The boy had an active social life.

All of this left me with a lot of alone time. I had to keep focused. After waking up just before seven, I started each morning with toast and coffee and a few sections of one of the three newspapers I had delivered. I then walked a few blocks to a yoga studio where I took a two-hour class. I ran errands on the way back and picked up sushi or a salad for lunch. I spent the afternoon going over my to-do list. I was looking for an acting class to join, taught by someone really good who would help me develop my skills. This was easier said than done. The well-known teachers had long waiting lists. There were plenty of amateur options but I didn't want to waste my time. I was also consulting with four possible decorators and trying to decide which one I wanted to hire. I couldn't decide what kind of change I wanted to make to the apartment but I was hungry for one.

The last items on my to-do list were about Ian. Since he died, I had found myself spending idle hours Googling him, trying to put his life together like pieces from a jigsaw puzzle. I couldn't entirely trust my memory on the particulars. The backup documentation helped my sense of security. My dining room table had grown a small mound of paperwork that I had ordered, hoping something might jump out at me. I had plumbed the Internet and the recesses of my own mind to put together a timeline.

Here's what I knew:

Ian and his sister were born and raised near San Francisco. Their father came from the South, had a military background, and had settled into a civil service job after leaving the Coast Guard. His parents married young and eventually divorced.

Online, I found an old interview in *Soap Opera Digest* after Ian was cast on *Wild Hearts*. He spoke about his early days in LA, living with a group of actors. He talked about riding his motorcycle through Malibu Canyon at night, past the spectacular houses in the Malibu Hills, dreaming of what might be. He also mentioned in the interview that he was engaged during those years. I had found no marriage certificate from that time and no evidence of the woman.

There was quite a bit of publicity about Ian when *Wild Hearts* started in September 1996. Most of it repeated the basic facts: he was a California boy who loved motorcycles, had his pilot's license, and had done some modeling. There was another uptick in publicity when Ian married Jasmine on Labor Day 1997. The publicity dropped off after that. Any subsequent articles I had found were usually tie ins to the show. Ian was interviewed about his current plotlines and hinting at what was to come.

Ian's family had taken on a peculiar fascination for me. I wondered about his mother. She seemed to be permanently absent from the family. She had not been at Ian's memorial. I had met Ian's sister briefly at his memorial. She was active on social media. Daisy hadn't mentioned their mother in any of the Facebook and Instagram posts I had seen. There had presumably been little or no contact since she had left when Ian was nine and Daisy seven.

Veruca had told me that Johanna Ray was incarcerated. I had scoured the Internet but had found no record of it. She had also told me that she had run into Esther and Ian a few times over the previous summer.

I had begun to brainstorm other possible other sources of information. After Googling New York therapists and leaving some unanswered voice mails, I decided to contact Peter's and my old therapist, the one we'd seen when Riley was six. We hadn't liked her much, but I thought her knowledge of my situation might help contextualize everything that had happened.

Her name was Meredith Goodwin. She was still in practice on Bank Street. When she returned my call, her breathy voice rankled. It took me back to those days, with Peter and me sitting on a couch with her opposite us, sizing us up with her ice blue eyes.

"I don't normally reengage with clients," she said after I reintroduced myself and reminded her that we had seen her for a few months back in 2004. "May I ask why you want to resume therapy with me and not someone else?"

I explained that, if she had held onto her notes, her knowledge of my history could serve as a shortcut. I wasn't sure I wanted to go over all the particulars again with a stranger. I also hoped to move quickly and a new therapist would need more time to build a foundation. "And you were good," I said. This was an outright lie. I hadn't been impressed with her at all.

She agreed to meet me, in part because I was available to come in the late morning, typically her slowest time. Walking down Bank Street, moving quickly to not be late for our 11:00 appointment, I felt a tingle of nerves like I sometimes did before an audition. I guess this would be a performance, of sorts.

I was a few minutes late, but she still kept me in the waiting room longer than I expected. I picked up a copy of *National Geographic* and paged through it. Finally, at 11:10 she appeared, wearing billowy black pants and a turquoise blouse. She still had that perfectly coiffed short blonde hair and slender, toned body. A diamond sparkled from the fourth finger of her left hand. I walked past her into the familiar tans and browns of an academic office. Her bookcases were lined with psychology textbooks. I had seen on her website that she had a PhD from Stanford and had published three books on eating disorders.

"I was reviewing my records from our previous sessions. It's been eleven years. May I ask how you and Peter have been?"

She took a seat opposite me with a legal pad and a Mont Blanc pen. "If you don't mind, I'm going to take some notes today to update your file."

I nodded.

"So," she said pausing for effect. "How are you?"

I had forgotten that this was her signature opening line. She had done it at the start of every session with Peter and me.

When I spoke, I was surprised that there was a catch in my voice. I felt tears sting my eyes. "I think my friend was killed. I think I may have had something to do with it."

~

For the first thirty minutes, all I did was talk: a rapid-fire monologue about Peter and me, about Italy, about the shock of Ian's death, about Catharine Nash and Sebastian Detlefsen, about my tense encounter with Esther Oden that day at Ithaca College in August, about the tidbits Veruca had fed to me about her since then. I had thought this would take session after session to unpack, but I found that by the time I had summarized it all, there were still nearly twenty minutes left. When I stopped, pausing for breath, tears streaming down my cheeks, Dr. Goodwin was staring at me impassively. Her face was tranquil, like a pond before a stone is skipped over its surface.

"You're going through a lot, Maggie, and I commend you for focusing on your mental health. But if I may, I might like to challenge you a bit on your logic." Her lips crinkled into a smile.

I waited for her to continue.

"Anyone going through an empty nest knows that it feels like an unacknowledged death. And now you've got another death to contend with, a literal one, and a divorce that has been a long time coming. In our past sessions, I recall that you didn't have very solid coping mechanisms."

Here it was: the quality I hadn't liked about her. She was a little too blunt for my tastes.

"Ian was a very important part of your life once. You never had any kind of closure to that. It's no wonder that you have pulled up all this guilt about it."

"Guilt?" I said.

"People engage in all kinds of strange sexual encounters. There are days when I hear about nothing but sex. What you and Ian did with Esther wasn't really that unusual. You may have violated some professional boundaries, but it's nothing to be carrying around so heavily."

"She seemed very angry with me the day I saw her," I said.

"Well, we don't know what she was angry about, though. She may just not want a reminder of a dark corner of her life. May I ask you what compelled you to drive up to Ithaca?"

"I wanted her to know about Ian," I said. "For some reason, I felt an obligation to tell her."

"Why?" she said.

"Well, there is something more to the story," I said.

Dr. Goodwin laughed lightly. "There always is."

I let that linger in the air. I didn't feel like spilling all my secrets today.

"What about what Veruca saw?" I asked her. "She said they looked like lovers."

Meredith – Dr. Goodwin – cocked her head to the side. "How well do you know Veruca?"

I told her we had worked together for fifteen years. She didn't seem to like anyone. I didn't know much about her personal life other than the fact that she was tight with Julian Barker.

"Why do you put such faith in what she says? You are accepting her comments as fact. If she hadn't seen Esther in years I'm not sure she could have even recognized her. People make mistakes in identification all the time. I was once convinced I saw my brother-in-law in a Whole Foods in Union Square. He lives in Phoenix so it made no sense. Vision begins to decline at midlife. You could have had eyes like a hawk for forty years and then one day you can't trust what's in front of you."

Dr. Goodwin wasn't convinced of Veruca's testimony. I wondered how this puzzle held up without those pieces in it. I tried to subtract them from my mind, focus on what I had firsthand knowledge of. What if Esther hadn't seen Ian since the summer of her internship? Did that change anything? I had still witnessed her anger that day in August. She didn't seem to be fully over what we had done to her.

I glanced at the clock. It was on a nightstand next to a box of tissues and a glass of water Dr. Goodwin had poured for me. We had about five minutes left.

"There's one other thing," I said. I had already summarized the party Catharine Nash had hired me for. I talked about how authentic the set seemed and about the diary entries. I pulled out my phone and showed her the snap I had taken of the note from Jacoby to Mira.

Dr. Goodwin pulled out her eyeglasses. She read and then reread it.

"What does this mean to you, Maggie? It's obviously important to you. What do you think it says?"

"I don't think Ian killed himself," I said. "I think he wrote this note in the hopes that someone would figure out he was being poisoned."

"Why couldn't he warn you in a more conventional way?"

Was I being foolish? Dr. Goodwin's placid face hid a sting of judgment behind it. I was sure that she didn't believe me. She probably thought I was working through my unexamined grief by creating a fairy tale. Perhaps I had made a mistake by confiding in her.

"I don't know," I said. "But until I feel satisfied with the facts, I am going to keep digging."

"It's your right to do that, Maggie. You'll know when the time is right to stop."

I felt absolved, like a priest had just given me my penance for the week. *Say five Hail Mary's and sin no more.* Maybe Dr. Goodwin wasn't so bad after all.

I got up and left her office, a feeling of resolve calcifying. I knew what I had to do next.

CHAPTER FIFTEEN

THEN

Julian Barker was our creator, our god. She had grown up in the Bronx, watching soap operas with her babysitter while her parents worked at the local chocolate factory.

After a college internship at *Search for Tomorrow*, Julian was hired as a writer's assistant on *All My Children*. On weekends, she would skateboard through Central Park, working out story ideas in her head. She stayed up most nights typing into her word processor, dreaming up new worlds. After a few years, she pitched an idea she had to the head writer at *AMC*, who passed it along to the executives. The bible for *Wild Hearts* was purchased. The powers that be took a gamble and it paid off: the first two seasons of the show rated higher than most of the soaps Julian had watched as a child. She was in charge and the show was her life.

Julian told us that her office door was always open to us. We all took advantage of it, stopping in to gripe about each other privately or about a story we didn't like or about the director who kept us after midnight every time she worked. She took it all in, her face conveying understanding. She was on our side.

The Monday after my night with Ian and Esther, I knew what I had to do. I stopped by her office during the afternoon, avoiding the frenzied energy of the morning, and shut the door behind me. She had a babbling stone display on a coffee table and a bookshelf full of awards behind her desk. She was just back from a two-week vacation on Martha's Vineyard and seemed happy to see me. I took a seat opposite her.

She said kindly, "So what can I help you with today?"

I thought of the previous weekend, the devilish pleasure on Ian's face as Esther emerged from the closet. Her ecstasy as Ian fucked her.

"It's that intern, Esther," I said. "Something happened."

Julian's face clouded a bit. She had not been expecting that reply.

"About a week ago, I invited her out for coffee. As you may recall, she found out about the internship through Barnard, my alma mater."

"I didn't know that," Julian said. The crow's feet near her eyes crinkled, as if she were deep in thought.

"It was meant to be a courtesy follow up, but we got to talking about other things. And she said something to me that was not appropriate. It made me very uncomfortable."

"Can you tell me more?" she asked.

"We were talking casually about the show and Barnard. I made some self-deprecating comment about getting older. She said to me, 'You're beautiful. You could turn me into a lesbian.' "

Julian looked bemused.

"I didn't feel comfortable. And since then it's just gnawing at me. Just the thought of dropping by the writers' office and seeing her is unpleasant."

"Are you sure you're not just overreacting?" Julian asked. "I said so many awkward things when I was that age. I'm lucky I got second chances."

"I have a right to feel safe on the set," I said. "Don't I?"

"How much longer is her internship?" Julian said, swiveling her neck to consult a wall calendar. It was mid-August.

"I think school starts after Labor Day."

"You might not interact with her much. I could have Veruca bring anything you need to the set or your dressing room."

"I really want her gone," I said. "It is not OK that she talked to me that way."

"I agree with you," Julian said. I knew she would. "She has burned a bridge. I will call Veruca first thing. Consider her gone by the end of the day. She can forget about the glowing reference we were going to give her, too. Mistake made, lesson learned."

I left the office with a spring in my step. My main obstacle was out of the way. Esther would be gone and I would have Ian all to myself. Little did I know that a few weeks later, everything would implode.

CHAPTER SIXTEEN

NOW

It was about an hour's drive from the Upper East Side to Williston Park where the precinct was located. I blasted the Doors as I drove. It was the same song I used to listen to before a love scene with Ian. *Come on Come on Come on now touch me babe. Can't you see that I am not afraid? What was that promise that you made?* I loved the raw sexuality of Jim Morrison's vocal and the building organ bridge. Pure bliss.

I was early so I pulled into the downtown area and drove around to get a sense of it. The main street had stores and a library and an old-time ice cream and candy shop. It was charming, a bit like I remembered Sea Cliff, albeit for a slightly less well-heeled crowd. The police station was just beyond the main drag, with a marquee announcing that it was the 3rd District of Nassau and a grey brick exterior. There was a window in front that brought to mind a piece of '50s art nouveau. It appeared to be unchanged since those days.

The interior had the same art deco aesthetic. I was feeling a little high, like I was about to step in front of a camera on a TV set. The woman behind the front desk had a tower of curly blonde hair piled on top of her head and a gold necklace around her neck that told me her name was *Angela*. Or maybe it said *Angel.*

"Detective Shimada will be right out," she said in a broad island accent, pointing one French nail at a set of plastic chairs in the sitting area. I took a seat and waited. After a few minutes, an attractive young woman with a short pixie cut and runner's body appeared through a set of glass doors. She was wearing a loose fitting pair of slacks and a white blouse.

"Maggie Grayson?" She asked me. I was taken out of the moment with the realization that this was Lou Shimada and that she was a woman. There hadn't been a picture on the website. She was about thirty with a smoky voice that reminded me a bit of Jasmine.

"Yes," I said.

"You can come with me." I followed her back through the glass doors past a group of desks to a conference room. I declined her offer of something to drink. She took a seat opposite me.

"First thing I have to tell you is that this conversation may be recorded," she said. "Precinct policy. What can I help you with today, Maggie?"

"I'm here about a death that occurred in your district. Ian Dorrit died in Sea Cliff recently. I believe it was ruled a suicide."

Lou had pulled out a pen and wrote something in a notebook. Her fingers were long and skinny like sticks.

"I've heard of this. He was a former soap star. He died by poisoning." She squinted at me. Something told me she knew plenty about Ian.

"Yes. I worked with him for many years on a soap called *Wild Hearts.*"

Lou's thin lips crinkled into a smile. I sensed she was having a little fun at my expense. She was just the right age to have watched the show during her college years. Did she recognize me?

"I have my doubts that it was a suicide. I'm wondering if there is any way for me to make a request to have his case reviewed."

Lou leaned forward in her chair. I could smell a faint whiff of perfume. "Well, Ms. Grayson, you should know that we as the police are trained to spot signs of foul play. If the assigned unit suspects a break-in or staged break-in at the death scene, or if we look into life insurance records and the will and something seems off, we will make that determination. All of that was done in this case, as is routine."

"And you found nothing?"

"If we had, an investigation would have been ordered. It would have been ruled a suspicious death. That didn't happen in this case."

"But if you discover something new, you would consider re-opening the case?"

"Of course. If we review at the information and determine that it is legitimate, we could re-open the case. Is there any new evidence you would like to present to me today?"

"Well, it's just Ian had a pretty colorful love life. I think he may have pissed off the wrong person."

"Tell me more about that."

"Well, he had a way of pushing boundaries. He made women do things that they didn't exactly want to do."

"Are you saying that he violated the law in any way? Do you know the definition of sexual assault?"

"Yes, I do," I said. "I don't think he ever crossed those lines. But I do think he made enemies."

"If you have any kind of proof that someone threatened him: a text, an email, a voice mail. Any of that I could consider."

I pulled out my phone and opened my Instagram feed. I hadn't posted anything since the shot of Peter and me with our large pasta bowls near the Spanish Steps. I pointed out a comment under the snap. *I'm a fan of the show. Where's Jacoby?*

I scrolled back a few weeks before the Italy shot. There was a snap of Riley and me holding up our playbills for *Hamilton*. We were seated at a cafe near the theater, coffee cups in front of us. We had just seen the show and had the enraptured glow of two people whose worldview had just been altered by artistic brilliance. Underneath there was another comment from the same poster. *I'm a fan of the show. Where's Jacoby?*

"May I take a picture of this?" She asked. When I nodded, she pulled out a phone and took a few snaps.

"How often do you get strange messages from fans like this?"

"Sometimes on my Instagram feed. Our characters had a huge following."

"*Ryano*," she said, reading the screen name of the poster. "Does that mean anything to you?"

I told her it did not.

Detective Shimada wrote something down. I had a sudden awareness that she would read my social media. I wondered if I should delete a few things. She had access to my police records, tax returns. I pulled my sweater around me. The air conditioning was unnaturally cold, like being in a walk-in freezer.

"See the problem is, these comments are not a credible threat. If it were something more explicit, we could consider spending the funds to trace where they came from."

I took back my phone and scrolled through until I found the picture of the diary entry. I explained where I had found it.

"What is the name of the man behind these parties?"

I gave her Sebastian's name and she wrote it down.

"Let me look into it. I'll be in touch if we need to talk further."

"Can I be in touch if I find something more significant?"

"Anytime. Is there anything else I can help you with today, Ms. Grayson?"

She fixed me with her soft hazel eyes. Her lips were thin and pink. She was somehow an amalgam of feminine and masculine. I wondered where she lived, and with whom.

"No, nothing," I said, and Detective Shimada got up and showed me out. As we parted, she handed me her business card. On the inside of her wrist, she had a tattoo. It was an infinity circle.

When I left the precinct, I got in my car and checked my messages. The first was from Peter. I had promised my son on Labor Day that he could remove a ceiling panel from his childhood bedroom. He and his father were going to come over and retrieve it. When Riley was seven, and obsessed with astronomy, Peter had painted a starry night image on the roof in his room. It hung above his bed like a mobile. Now that he was on his own, Riley wanted to turn it into a wall painting. Peter had sent a second text that he wanted to clear out the camping equipment that we owned. When Riley was little and obsessed with night skies, we had bought a bunch of equipment and then used it only a handful of times. It had been sitting in storage since.

Tell me a good time for us to stop by. His last text read.

I scrolled past that, making a mental note to follow up on it later. The next was a voice mail from Catharine Nash. Sebastian Detlefsen was hosting another party in three weeks, this time with a scene between Mira and Valentina. Would I be interested in doing another performance? The same wage rates applied.

When I pulled into the parking garage, my mind was awash in thoughts. I breezed past Edgar, who was sitting with an ear bud in his ear, following some sports match. I pantomimed a hello.

He pulled out his ear bud. "Miss Grayson, a package was delivered for you. Actually it's for your guest." He got up from his seat and went into a back room. When he reemerged, he had a brown box on a handcart.

"It's heavy," he said. "It's starting to fall apart."

I hit the button and the elevator doors dinged open. Edgar rolled the cart in and we rode to the eleventh floor, chatting amiably. When we reached my unit, I hit the door code and directed him to leave the box on the floor of Riley's room.

I moved around the apartment, stripping my bed and collecting the linen from the master bedroom. I went into Riley's room. Corey had made his bed that morning but I grabbed his sheets, crumpling them into a ball with the others. As I walked out of the room, I noticed the return address on the box that had been delivered. Jasmine had sent over what I assumed to be the remains of Corey's stuff during his months housesitting for her. I walked back through the kitchen to the spare bedroom. There was a washer and dryer, an ironing board, and a desk with a computer there. There was also a small bed for overnight visitors, which was currently heaped with shopping bags.

I threw the load into the washing machine along with a pod. When I walked back into the foyer, I noticed that Riley's light was still on. I walked over. On the floor near the box, something had fallen out. When I bent down I saw that there was a tear in the base of the box about the size of a silver dollar. On the carpet near the hole was a small zip drive. It was a pretty pastel blue. I grabbed it and stuck it on top of the box.

I went back to my living room and flipped open my copy of *The Sisters Rosensweig*. When I was preparing my audition a few weeks ago, I had felt drawn into the story and was reading it now for pleasure. The events of the play took place at a birthday get together in London. The characters were three adult sisters from Brooklyn. It was sophisticated humor. I wasn't sure that I got all of it.

After I had read for a bit, I got up and stretched. I was hungry, but it was still a good hour from supper. I wandered back to the guest room and put the load of laundry into the dryer. I thought again of the blue pastel zip drive. I knew I shouldn't look. But the need for a distraction pulled me back to Riley's room. I grabbed the zip drive, feeling my heart rate accelerate. Why was I nervous? There was no way Corey would know I had snooped.

When I got back to the laundry room, I turned on the computer and let it warm up. I took a seat and put the drive in. I clicked on the finder tab and opened the contents. There were a slew of pictures of Corey in drag: torch singer, cowgirl, chanteuse. A few videos were in the row below: drag performance pieces, audition practice, and so on. I scrolled down further. These rows had similar content. Corey had evidently been writing a one-man show about being a homeless queer teen in New Orleans. I watched a few pieces. They were still pretty rough but he had some good content.

I scrolled further down, drawn by the image of a poster I recognized. It was a close up of James Stewart's face with aviator goggles on his head. It was a movie from the 1950s in which he played Charles Lindbergh. It was a still shot from a video. I clicked on it and unmuted the volume. The camera panned from the movie poster across an apartment. There were two men in costume sitting on barstools making conversation. As the camera pulled back, I recognized the set. It resembled the apartment Corey's character had lived in on *Wild Hearts*. There was a knock on the door and one of the actors got up and answered it. A young man in a leather jacket entered. At first I didn't recognize him, but more closely it was unmistakable: it was Ian. The three men continued to banter. This wasn't an old episode of the show. The two other actors were strangers to me.

The story continued, dramatically. One of the men pulled a knife on Ian and in the next scene he was tied up with rope in a chair in the living room. The larger of the two men, the alpha, gently moved the tip of his knife against Ian's chin.

"What would you do to be free?" he asked.

"Anything," Ian said, his face with the knife in close up.

The music switched to cheesy disco. They were in a different room, a bedroom, with a mirror ball on the ceiling. Ian's character was bound to the bed. He was wearing small leopard print underwear that showed off his bulge.

I continued watching, mesmerized and horrified. The two men were humiliating Ian. When it got to be too much, too real, I ejected the drive and powered down my computer. I moved back into the kitchen, feeling like I was returning from a foreign place. I didn't know what to make of what I had just seen or why Corey had this in his possession. And because of how I had found it, there was no way I could ask. I returned the zip drive to Riley's room and shut the door firmly as I left.

That night, I had a strange dream. There was a flash of lightning in my bedroom and I woke to find Esther standing at the end of my bed. She was holding Oswald, the fluffy orange cat I had adopted after graduating Barnard. I had him for years; he died when Riley was ten. In the dream, Esther was whispering in Oswald's ear. As I sat up to try to discern the words, Oswald hissed at me, as loud as the clap of thunder that accompanied it. I woke up in a sweat, disarmed, too disturbed to fall back asleep.

The symbolism was not lost on me. It reminded me a bit of the performance I had done for Sebastian Detlefsen. In that script, there is a scene in which Mira is undressing in her bedroom. She doesn't know that Duncan, dressed in Jackie O sunglasses and a turquoise silk headscarf, is standing outside her window. I thought of that comment scrawled in the back of the prop diary. Was it possible that Ian had some connection to Sebastian? Maybe Catharine Nash had approached Ian over the summer and their first party had had a scene with Ian. They could have hired someone else to play Mira. Maybe Ian didn't want to work with me again.

It occurred to me, though, that the scene bore some resemblance to the shadow game that Ian liked to play. Could there be a connection somehow? It was one of those thoughts that overwhelmed me slightly. I wasn't sure I could make sense of it.

I peeked in Riley's room. Corey hadn't come home. This wasn't unusual. He and his friends still went to clubs and sang karaoke and crashed on each others' couches. I envied their eternal youth. I wandered around my apartment, turning the kitchen TV on to keep me company.

I flipped around the channels, hoping for anything that could take my mind off the present. I settled on a Hitchcock marathon. I caught the tail end of *The 39 Steps* and then settled in for *Psycho.*

It occurred to me as the story unfolded just how much Duncan Wilder was like Norman Bates. Julian was a bit of a copycat. I guess it follows that Mira was a bit like Marion Crane, unaware that she was being surveilled. All that was missing from our plotline was a shower scene.

I continued watching the movie until the sun came up. I had the filmy, greasy feel of a night of indulgence. I switched off the TV, ground some coffee beans, set the coffeemaker and wandered back into my bedroom. Outside my window, in the apartments across the way, I could see a businessman in a starched white shirt putting on his tie and watching the morning news. One story up, a housekeeper dusted around plant pots on a windowsill, a tabby cat lounging nearby.

I ran the shower for a few minutes, then stripped and got under the hot spray. What a luxury to linger for a moment, the steam and water both invigorating and soothing. I filled a washcloth with body wash, scrubbing off the night, and ran a few fingers of shampoo through my wet hair.

I thought of the porn video I had seen and of the box in Riley's room. What more might I learn if I cracked it open? It was in my apartment. I could unpack the box and recycle it and Corey would be none the wiser. But, then, what if Jasmine raised the issue?

Another thought percolated as I ran a bit of conditioner through my hair. The set in the porn movie looked a hell of a lot like Olli's apartment on *Wild Hearts.* I was present at the final cast party five years before and watched the sets be torn down. It was impossible that someone had kept that set intact. Had the filmmakers hired someone from the show to design for them? I hadn't seen Lara Stone since the Sebastian Detlefsen performance, but I had always had a friendly relationship with her.

I turned the water off, rubbing my hair dry and wrapping another towel around me. I pulled on some string pants and a t-shirt, padded into the kitchen, poured myself a mug of coffee, and walked to the living room. I pulled open my laptop and fired it up. I took a seat, drinking the bitter morning brew, and waited for my screen to come to life. I hit the bookmarks bar and opened Facebook.

A Friend search turned up half a dozen people named Lara Stone, including one with whom I had seventeen friends in common. I clicked on her profile picture, which was a shot of the Brooklyn Bridge. I scanned the list of our friends in common: Ty Harris, Veruca St. Clair, Julian Barker. This had to be her.

I sent her a friend request. Within minutes, she accepted it. Then I opened a message and typed. *Hey stranger. It was great running into you at Mr. Detlefsen's party. I was wondering if you might like to get a drink or coffee sometime? A catch up is sounding pretty good right about now.*

I sat back, took another sip of coffee, and considered the note. Was I being too forward, too familiar? I deleted the salutation and replaced it with her first name. Then I read it again and hit send.

CHAPTER SEVENTEEN
NOW

When I got back from yoga the next day, my phone started buzzing as I was waiting for the elevator. I was expecting to hear from Catharine Nash, as I hadn't yet returned her phone call. I felt a slight ambivalence about going deeper into that process, especially since I still wasn't sure what to make of that journal entry. Did Ian write that, thinking I might see it? If so, he must have been involved in another production. And what did it mean?

Instead I found a different number on my screen. I hit answer.

"Maggie, it's Jasmine."

I would recognize that smoky voice anywhere.

"I'm just getting on an elevator. I might cut out," I said, stepping on and hitting eleven. I could hear sounds of the street on the other end and faint footfalls. It sounded like Jasmine was walking down the street.

"I got an infinity circle card," Jasmine said. "Someone slipped it through my door slot. I thought I would check with you before I answered it."

I hit the door code and entered my apartment.

"The number belongs to a woman named Catharine Nash," I said. "She works for a guy named Sebastian Detlefsen who made a lot of money in tech. He hosts parties where they recreate episodes from the show. Lara Stone is involved, and Julian Barker. It's easy money."

"Well, see, here's the thing, Maggie, I was at a party over the weekend and I asked some of the actors there if they had ever heard of this. One of them said he had and he warned me about it."

"Warned you?"

"Yeah, my friend Sly Gatewood. Do you remember him? He played Lucky on *All My Children*. He said that he did a party for them and it was a really bad experience. I couldn't' really get him to elaborate. It was like he wanted to warn me but he also didn't want to talk about it."

I thought of the journal entry. Was it possible they had approached Ian and something had gone wrong? I was feeling more and more like it was a possibility.

"It's funny you say that. I did one party for them and it was easy. And yet something weird did happen to me, too."

The street noises on the other end of the line had gone silent. I could hear Jasmine clomping around inside somewhere.

"Can you tell me about it?"

"It was one of the props on the set, a journal in Mira's bedroom. There was a note in it and I just had this strange feeling that Ian wrote it."

"Ian? You think he was involved with this?"

"I can't say for sure. Maybe I'm imagining things. But, Jasmine, do you have a minute to talk about Ian?"

"Sure," she said. A refrigerator door opened and there were sounds of her drinking something.

"Did he ever seem suicidal to you, when you were close?"

"No, never. He was a bit moody at times, but what actor isn't? But he had demons. His mother, for one."

"I don't remember him ever talking about his mother, other than the fact that she left when he was nine."

"It was something he held very close to his vest. It came up when we were talking about having a baby. He was deeply ambivalent because he was afraid of the kind of father he would be."

"Did you get any other sense of his mother? Any detail?"

"Surprisingly little. He said that his parents split up when he was nine and that his father raised him and his sister. His father joined some weird church that thought women should be subservient to men. Ian told me he grew up going to this church that had a room painted to look like the

Garden of Eden. They had weekly services where they would talk about how women had been created to be the man's helper."

It sounded like Ian's parents were polar opposites, including their theological beliefs.

I wasn't sure how much of my research to divulge to Jasmine. I didn't want to seem like I was obsessed with Ian, especially to someone with whom I shared this peculiar history.

"Do you remember anything else he said about his mother?"

"The subject always came up in strange ways. For instance, I once said I wanted to see Bob Dylan in concert and he refused. He said it was because it reminded him of his mother. I guess she was a fan and it was too painful for him. Also he and his sister had a tradition of spending Mother's Day together. Ian would fly out to San Francisco and they would do something together. I thought it was kind of nice, actually. It seemed like a healthy way to heal."

"So what do you think you're going to do about Catharine Nash?" I asked. "Maybe pitch the card?"

"I'm kind of curious," Jasmine said. "If both of the people I know have had weird experiences, what might happen to me?"

"We could agree to do it together," I suggested. "Just one last time. Use it as a kind of control."

"What kind of money are we talking?"

"They gave me ten grand for four hours' work. It was deposited into my checking account within three days."

"It seems silly to turn down easy money," she said. "Plus I get to be Valentina again. I have missed her."

"So, you in?"

Jasmine exhaled blithely. "Why the hell not?"

Later that day, when the doorbell rang and I opened the door, I was hit by the memory of all the years Peter and I had shared this space. He appeared in the foyer wearing a blue dress shirt rolled up to his elbows and a pair of ironed jeans. His brown hair was cut short, a few flecks of gray visible.

"You look very handsome," I said reflexively. I was feeling kind for the moment.

"You too, darling," my estranged husband said and leaned over to swipe my cheek with a kiss. Riley was right behind him.

I was in and out of Riley's room and the kitchen, trying to assist them while I organized dinner. As I was chopping some tomatoes for a salad, they inched by with the panel in their hands. There was a service elevator just outside the kitchen door that led to the basement storage and also a parking garage. They were gone for a while as they took the panel down to Peter's car. He had bought another Audi now that we were living apart.

I poured myself some wine. I pulled the clay pot out of the oven and basted the chicken with butter and spices. There were dumplings and vegetables in broth surrounding it. I could smell parker house rolls baking. This was one of Riley's favorite meals.

We had about twenty minutes until the chicken was ready, so when the guys returned, Peter and I exited by the back door and took the service elevator down eleven floors to the basement. When the doors parted we were in a dark open space. It had an industrial, utilitarian quality. I hit the lights to reveal thirty mesh cages of various sizes with red numbers hanging above each. We found our way to 11B and went inside.

"I've been meaning to ask you something," I said, as he rooted in boxes and unzipped bags. "Early on in our marriage, I found condoms in your suitcase. Are you ready to own up that?"

My husband sighed. "Maggie, we've been getting along so well. Must you?"

"I won't be mad. I'm just trying to close the door on all this."

"One of these days, Maggie, you're going to be hit from the sky with the knowledge that I wasn't the one who pulled out of this marriage. You alienated me after Riley was born. And, yes, I crossed a few lines once or twice. I'm not proud of it. But why does it matter at this juncture?"

I was feeling sensitive to his criticism and to his revelation. Maybe asking about it had been a bad idea.

We continued rooting around for a while. Together we pulled down the kayak, which was hanging from the mesh ceiling. We stacked up a tent, sleeping bags, a camping stove, a hanging lamp.

Peter got busy opening and riffling through boxes. I absently opened an old hat box and found Ziploc bags full of black and white photographs. Peter's mother had given us these family photos before she died. I had meant to figure out who everyone was, maybe frame a few, but the project had fallen by the wayside. Now that they were no longer my family, it seemed pointless.

"What are you looking for?"

"College stuff," he said. "I probably would have written the dates here somewhere."

"So this would have been 1984-88?" I said, trying to be helpful. I hadn't known Peter then and had only heard snatches of stories here and there. He had pledged a fraternity and majored in economics. He had a steady girlfriend who went on to med school.

"I think I've got it here," Peter said, taking out a box to the best available light. He rummaged around a bit and cursed. "Dammit. I wonder what Mother did with my yearbooks. They don't seem to be here."

Peter closed the box back up and pulled the string light off. I shut the door and locked it behind us. "If you come across a box with my high school stuff, let me know. College too."

"Will do."

"Please be careful, Maggie. I do worry about you here alone."

"I'm not alone, Peter. Corey is staying with me. You going to be OK loading up the car?"

"Yes. See you upstairs."

We walked back past the mesh cages, other people's lives in shadows, and parted at the service elevator. Peter walked to the parking garage with the first load of stuff. I stepped into the elevator and rode it up. I entered the kitchen to find Riley sitting at the kitchen table, scrolling through this phone.

"I hope you're staying for dinner," I asked him.

"Hell yes," he said. "It smells like home."

I reflexively checked my phone. There was a message there.

Ms. Grayson, this is Detective Lou Shimada from the 3rd Precinct. Please call me back at your earliest convenience.

I hit redial and slipped into my bedroom. There was a sliding door that shut off the sounds of the apartment. As the phone rang on her end, my heart began to beat more loudly.

"Thanks for calling me back," she said. "I did some research after you stopped by the other day. I found out some information about Ian's mother. Johanna Ray was found guilty of statutory rape. She is currently incarcerated in New York State. Not eligible for parole until 2025."

"A woman can go to prison for rape?"

"Under certain circumstances, yes. You said that Johanna left the family when Ian was ten?"

"I think he was nine," I said. I only knew bits and pieces of Ian's childhood. I remembered the story about the day she left. He was up in the branches of the apple tree and his last image of her was watching his father hit his mother. As far as I knew, it was their last contact.

"Also you said that the man who gave you the business card was named Sebastian Detlefsen?"

"Yes."

"I can't say much, but I would encourage you to stay away from him."

"Why?"

"His ex-wife and his ex-girlfriend both have restraining orders against him."

I saw her point. One ex you could write off as a kook but two was trouble.

After we hung up, I served up dinner for Riley, Peter, and me in flat soup bowls. Soon we were eating around the dining room table, a new family. I tried to stay engaged with the conversation and with the food, but my mind was crowded with other thoughts. I felt a growing certainty that I was on the cusp of the missing information that would provide clarity about Ian's death. I just wasn't sure what it was or where it would lead me.

CHAPTER EIGHTEEN
NOW

The coffee shop was called Remedy. It was one of these hipster coffee bars that serve $10 donuts and make each cup of coffee by single drip. It was in a trendy section of Brooklyn Heights, wedged between a half-block on either side of red brick row houses. Lara had suggested the location when she had responded to my Facebook message a few days before. We agreed to meet for coffee at midday. As my subway car pulled into Brooklyn, I was hit by a wave of nostalgia for the *Wild Hearts* days. In the first few seasons, when I still lived in Greenwich Village, I had often hopped on a D train in the early morning, my hair up in a cap, and rode through the borough to the studio. I got recognized sometimes, but less than I might have liked. Soap opera actors were only marginally famous.

Remedy had a slanted roof and box windows and, in the interior, a turntable with stacks of vinyl near the coffee bar. I was early so I shifted through the albums, past Patti Smith and The Sugar Cubes and The Pixies, before I settled on Pavement. We had listened to this a lot on the set and I loved one of the tracks. I put the needle on the groove and "Trigger Cut" filled the room.

The barista behind the counter eyed me disdainfully as I took a place in line. He kept talking to a woman who was waiting for her serving.

"It's the slow death of critical thinking," he said to her, wiping out a coffee cup with a rag. "He's emboldening morons to think they're smarter than the elites. I blame the DNC for this whole thing."

"I thought this was a Bernie-free zone," the voice came from behind me, a soft Southern lilt. I turned to find Lara Stone behind me, dressed in a red silk blouse and linen pants.

Chastened, he switched gears. "What can I get for you?"

"Whatever she's having," I said, gesturing behind me. I was paralyzed by indecision by the menu in front of me. It was as complex as a wine label. Lara ordered two Ethiopians with lavender and peet and a spinach croissant for herself. Isaac went to work. When the order was up, we walked through the interior to a garden outside. We each took a seat on a bench.

"I told Isaac if he keeps blaring his political opinions, I'm going to start wearing my Reagan button."

I ignored the comment. Politics bored me. Plus it was like the Oscars this year: everyone knew ahead of time who was going to win. In two weeks, we would have a woman president. For some reason, I didn't care.

"Did you know there are four waves to coffee?" Lara said. "This place bills itself as a fourth wave coffee joint."

"What are the others?" I said, sipping my mug of black Ethiopian.

"First wave was the mass production of stuff like Folger's that allowed regular folk to have their morning cups. Second wave was Starbucks, the designer trend of the '90s, and the third were its competitors. And now we've arrived at places like this, where everything is fair trade and done as an individual serving."

"It all seems a bit pretentious to me," I said, "but this garden seating is lovely." It was a weekday and we were alone amidst the bamboo trees and koi pond.

"This is my local place," Lara said, "They just opened about six months ago."

Lara had grown up in Charleston in a haunted antebellum house with a father who prosecuted unsavory criminals and a mother who had once been Miss South Carolina. She was an only child, spending the swamp heat summers reading thick books and taking breaks to draw and sketch. When you don't have any siblings to distract you, your imagination becomes your companion. She created the worlds that she wanted to live in.

"So what have you been doing since the show ended?" I asked. I remembered seeing her at the cast and crew farewell party.

"This and that," she said. "I've designed a few play sets. I was so busy working when the show was on that I socked away a lot of savings. It wasn't even virtuous; I just never had the time or energy to shop or travel. I'm thanking my lucky stars now."

"And you work for Sebastian Detlefsen?"

"Yeah, I've done a couple parties for him. He's a bit of a freak, but nothing unusual by show biz standards."

"I guess with enough money, the world is a sandbox."

"Apparently."

A bald man with gold hoop earrings had joined us in the garden, yakking on his cell phone while stirring milk into an iced coffee. He took a seat at a table a few feet from us.

"How about you, Maggie? What have you been doing?"

I filled her in on the synopsis of my last few years: the Tom Stoppard play, the auditions, the growing frustration that I might not work steadily again. She listened attentively, biting into her croissant occasionally. The bald man pulled out a laptop and put in ear buds.

"Listen, I wanted to ask you something," I said, pulling my phone out of my back pocket and scrolling through my videos. I turned the phone to her and hit play. She shielded the screen for shade and watched. It was muted.

"I heard Ian was doing porn before he died," I said, pulling the phone back when she seemed to have lost interest. "And that reminds me of your sets."

Lara fixed me with a solid stare. A cloud seemed to pass over her face, from friendly to guarded.

Acting quickly to smooth the tension, I said, "It's kind of embarrassing. But do you think you could hook me up?"

She stared at me a moment longer, then smiled noncommittally. "You looking for work, Maggie? I thought you were married to the prince of Wall Street."

"We're getting divorced. He's hired a killer to defend him." My first lie of the day.

"Alright, Maggie, I'll let you in. There is a secondary porn market that specializes in American actors. Kind of like those commercial markets that use A-list stars in Japan. You've seen *Lost in Translation*?"

I nodded. Celebrities made big bucks hawking products on the contractual condition that the commercials would never be seen anywhere outside of Asia. Apparently the market didn't end at advertisements or in Asia.

"I build sets for them sometimes. Ian was one of their regulars in the last few years. There is a big underground for this type of thing. Ian's movies were popular in some of our foreign markets."

I sat back, the late afternoon sun hitting my face. I reached into my purse and pulled out my sunglasses.

"Maggie, I have to warn you that these productions are strictly on demand. I can't guarantee you anything."

"Oh, maybe not then," I said.

"Well, if you're interested, I can maybe hook you up with an informational interview."

I blinked, waiting.

"Sebastian Detlefsen did not make his money in tech. That's just his cover story. He's the porn king of Denmark."

This was starting to make sense. Here was the link between Sebastian and Ian.

"How'd you find this, anyhow?" Lara asked, picking up her last croissant crumb with her moistened thumb. "It looks like an illegal download."

I wasn't sure if I could trust her with the truth.

"Ian's sister gave me a box of his belongings. It was sweet of her to think of me. I think this was included by mistake." A bold faced lie. My second in under five minutes. I was getting better at them.

"Well, thanks for meeting me," I said, "I should probably get back to the city before my subway turns into a pumpkin."

I stood up, a little wobbly on my heels, and reached over to hug her goodbye. I won't deny it; it felt good to have human contact.

I had some time to kill after I left the coffeehouse so I walked towards Cranberry Street. Near the water was the red brick house where they filmed *Moonstruck*. It was my mom's favorite movie. We had watched it every Christmas Day when I was growing up. I took a shot. "Snap out of it," I captioned my text. I knew she would catch the reference.

All these gestures I made for my mom were small efforts to gain her favor. It had been like this my whole life. Maybe I was drawn to acting because it made me the center of someone's world. I yearned, ached, for her attention even now. I was drawn to men like Ian and Peter who just didn't seem to care that much about me. I wondered if this could ever change.

And, yet, despite the sting of an imperfect life, I still felt gratitude for the childhood my mother had given me. I thought of Ian, at nine, waking up one day and realizing that his mother was gone for good. What was the impact of that kind of desertion? Did he ever trust another woman again?

I continued walking, lost in thought. I wasn't hugely surprised that Ian had done porn. He was a carnal person who had few inhibitions. He had grown accustomed to a certain lifestyle and porn may have offered easy money to keep pace with it. He was, however, not terribly comfortable around gay men. It was one of the reasons he and Corey had never gotten along very well. I wasn't sure why Corey had a copy of the film on his zip drive. Perhaps he was involved in porn as well, a supplement to his musical theater earnings? I wasn't sure how I could broach the topic, given how I had discovered it. I liked Corey and did not want to alienate him.

There was a nagging thought, though, that had come back to me several times since I found the zip drive. That day in my living room, when I was expressing guilt over what I had done to Esther, Corey had told me, " We have all done terrible things." He had seemed pretty nonchalant about it. Was it possible I couldn't trust him? Was it possible, even, that he had something to do with Ian's death? I wanted to believe otherwise.

CHAPTER NINETEEN
NOW

The night of the next performance, I arrived early. The neighborhood was hopping on a Saturday night. The same beefy Asian guy was seated on a folding chair near the elevator. When he sent me up this time, the elevator opened onto the roof. The party crew was in full swing. There were hanging lights and speakers and setting up small tables with chairs.

The set was near the edge of the roof, a replica of the Wilder dining room. Jasmine was standing near it, dressed in a tight Lycra dress and a leather jacket. Her long black hair had been ironed and she was wearing make-up. In the scene, which we had rehearsed the day before, Mira and Valentina had both been at a costume ball the night before. Valentina had walked in on an intimate scene between Mira and Jacoby. Since Mira was married to Joshua, Valentina's beloved older brother, there was some tension between them. We would basically insult each other for fifteen minutes and walk away with a hearty paycheck.

"We have a dressing cabana set up back there if you need it," Catharine Nash said as she sidled up. "I'd like you both to make your entrances from behind the set. I've got some water back there if you need anything while you wait. Don't forget we've got an open bar tonight as well."

The elevator dinged and Sebastian appeared. He was wearing a black dinner jacket and a top hat.

"So glad you could make it again," he said to me, giving me an air hug. "The crowd is expecting a catfight."

It was in the script: after our last line of dialogue, I was supposed to lunge at Valentina. Together we would freeze in place. That would be the end of the scene.

Sebastian continued talking, "In my family we have a saying, 'Honor among women is rarer than moonlight at midday.' "

I crinkled my nose to bat away his rudeness. Why was it that people wanted to see women as rivals? I had witnessed just as much pettiness between men over the years. Female solidarity was not an oxymoron.

He moved away, flying into a huddle with Catharine near the bar.

I thought of some snarky comment to lob at Jasmine but thought better of it. She was distracted anyway.

"Shall we go get out of sight?" I suggested to her. "I think the guests arrive at 9."

She was quiet, pensive.

"Is something the matter?" I asked her, moving closer. She muttered a few words that I couldn't quite make out. I asked her to repeat it.

"My mother said that," she said, her voice low. "After my father left us for one of her friends, she said, 'Honor among women is rarer than moonlight at midday.'"

I cast a glance over her shoulder. Sebastian had walked over to the elevator and was greeting the first of the guests. A group of Asian women, much like the crowd at the first event, were moving into the open space.

"Maybe it's a common axiom," I said. "It could be cross cultural."

Jasmine fixed me with a look that I had never seen from her before. Her face was that of a frightened child. "She didn't say it. She wrote it. It was her suicide note."

When our scene was finished, with me lunging at Valentina, the crowd began to clap. I took Jasmine's hand and we did a curtain call. What the audience didn't know was that Jasmine was completely off her game tonight. I had done many scenes like this with her over the years and I had never seen her so rattled. It was like acting with someone who is partially catatonic.

Catharine appeared with flutes of pink champagne, but I politely declined. I grabbed Jasmine by the hand and, after a few perfunctory introductions to guests, jumped in the elevator. She leaned back against the wall, spooked. I had not realized that Jasmine's mother was dead, or that she had taken her own life. There was a lot I didn't know about her. Maybe this explained her bond with Ian: they were both abandoned children.

"What was I thinking doing this?" she asked. "I guess I was just morbidly curious."

"I'm sorry about your mother," I said. "I didn't know."

"My mother got married just out of high school. She could have been an actress or dancer, but she chose to devote all her time to raising my sisters and me. Right before my senior year, my dad moved out. For a long time, I didn't know what had happened. But eventually it came out. He had fallen in love with my mom's closest friend. She was shattered. She never really recovered from the betrayal. When I was away at college, I got a call from my grandfather. My mother had overdosed on Xanax."

"I'm so sorry," I said.

"I was older when my mother died so I always felt that I was a little better equipped to deal with it. But it was still devastating."

I thought back to that note that Jesse had given us on the night of Ian's memorial. Was it possible Sebastian was behind it? And could he somehow have known about Jasmine's mother? It seemed unlikely. And yet experiencing this again was creepy.

"I want to talk to your friend," I said. "What was his name? Sly?"

Jasmine exhaled. "Right, Sly Gatewood. Didn't you ever watch *All My Children*?"

I could call up an image of Sly in my mind. I had seen him at the Emmys once. I wasn't sure I had ever watched his work, though.

"Not with any regularity," I said. The elevator reached the mezzanine and pinged. When we exited there was a small group of Japanese women waiting to get on. They talked excitedly back and forth. I didn't have the heart to tell them they were late and had missed the show.

"Sly seemed very uncomfortable when I brought this up. I don't recommend approaching him about it."

"Don't worry," I said, stepping out into the street. "I don't want to bother anyone."

I hugged her goodbye, telling her to call me if she needed anything. I wasn't sure when I would see her again, probably not soon. I had my own plan to meet Sly Gatewood that would be taking up my immediate time. With a little luck, it would work out.

CHAPTER TWENTY
NOW

Sly Gatewood lived in an apartment building near Washington Square, a complex that housed NYU faculty and alums. In the three days that I had been following him, I had learned a surprising amount about him. He left the building every morning at 7 and walked to a gym three blocks over. When he emerged two-and-a-half hours later, he was fresh and clean from a long workout and a shower. He then picked up coffee and a copy of *The Times* from a cafe about a half a block from his place. So, at least in the mornings, he was a creature of habit. This would make my task slightly easier.

I wasn't familiar with his work on *All My Children,* but a few Google searches gave me a general sense of his tenure there. His character was the owner of a nightclub that had ties to organized crime. From everything I read, Lucky was a likeable guy driven to extremes to support his family. He and his love interest on the show seemed to have a sizable fan base.

And somehow, Sly had gotten involved with Sebastian Detlefsen. After what Jasmine had told me, I was prepared for resistance but determined to talk to him. There was a bench in Washington Square Park opposite his building complex that gave me a decent view of the front entrance. Each morning I arrived just before seven with a cup of coffee and a copy of *The Girl on the Train.* I had read it in Italy and didn't much care for it, but it was the least heavy of the cloth books in Peter's office. I sat with it open, my coffee cup steaming nearby, and watched for the glass doors of his building to swing open.

On the fourth morning, his habits finally changed. Instead of heading north to the gym as he had the previous mornings, he walked south. Intrigued, I stood up from my bench and followed him at a safe distance. He was wearing a blue hoodie and black knit cap. I could just make him out bobbing along the pavement. After a few blocks, he turned abruptly and disappeared from my view. I quickened my pace as much as I could without arousing suspicion. When I caught up, I found him. He had stepped into an ATM vestibule.

He was leaning down towards someone who was obscured from my view by his large frame. There were red painted fingernails splayed on the back of his hoodie. I stepped closer, pulling out my ATM card, and stuck it in the entrance key. When I pulled the door, it was still locked.

The noise caused Sly and the woman to part. He reached over and pushed the door open so I could enter. He smiled abashedly at me as I entered. The woman he was with was barely five feet with a short blonde pixie haircut. She smiled at me shyly. Instantly, I recognized her: she had played wild child Millie Mack on *As The World Turns*. In the last few seasons of *Wild Hearts*, we had appeared at a few publicity events together.

"Gosh, I'm blanking on your name," she said. The voice was unmistakable: she had a broad Southern accent that she exaggerated on the show. "I just loved your work."

I threw a smile at both of them while I put my ATM card into the machine. It was critical that I made this seem as spontaneous as possible.

"Maggie Grayson," I said, kicking the friendly up to ten. "Didn't we sign autographs together upstate at the harvest fair?" I hit a few buttons and waited while the machine chuffed out four fifty-dollar bills. I stuck them in my book.

"That's right," she said. "You look great." She was undeniably cute and clearly smitten with her man. But why were they meeting in an ATM vestibule at seven in the morning?

"You live near here?" Sly asked me.

"I'm staying with my son," I lied. "My apartment is being painted so

I'm just trying to stay out of the way for a few days. But I think he's getting tired of me. I told him, 'you weren't tired for those nine months you were curled up inside of me.'"

Sly and his friend – I couldn't pull up her real name if I had ever known it – shook their heads amiably.

"Good seeing you," I said, breezing by and exiting in the direction of Thompson Street. I would need to keep up this ruse as long as necessary.

❧

The next morning, I knew I had to change my routine. I waited a little longer before taking the subway down to Washington Square Park at about 9. The car was packed with end-of-the-week stragglers, forcing themselves out of bed at the last acceptable minute. Their eyes were vacant as they read screens, scrolled through Kindles, rocked out to ear buds.

At about nine-thirty, I made my way to the coffee shop near Sly's gym. It was nearly empty after the morning rush. Tables were still cluttered with half-drunk lattes and discarded newspapers. I ordered an Americano and instant oatmeal and cleared off a table while the barista filled my order. I pulled out my book, skimming until my breakfast was served. The oatmeal was steaming. A few blueberries dotted the top. I took a spoonful and blew on it before eating.

A few minutes later, he appeared, shiny and clean from the gym shower.

"Sly, my man," the barista called out as he entered. He then reached over the coffee bar to do a man shake, something between a fist bump and a slithery snake. What was it with guys and their complicated greetings?

They chatted a bit while I pretended to read my book. I was focusing on a paragraph when Sly said to me, "Your kid kick you out?"

I smiled. "Entirely my choice," I said. "I've heard good things about this place." I took a sip of my Americano.

"I used to work here in my student days," he said, dropping his gym bag into a nearby vacant chair. In his online bio, it said that he was a graduate of the Tisch School of the Arts.

"So you and Kenzie, huh?" I said while he waited for his drink to be up. I had Googled them the night before. Her name was Kenzie Cooper and her Wikipedia entry showed that she had been married since 2013 to a stockbroker.

"Nothing to see there," he said, emitting a bray of laughter. Romance was complicated sometimes. Who was I to judge? At least he had a sense of humor about my pesky question.

"So I think we have a friend in common?" I said. "Jasmine Dakari?"

Sly was pouring a few drops of half and half into his double espresso. He stirred and nodded his head.

"Yeah, I've known her for years. We have the same acting coach."

"Ever been to one of her dinner parties?" I asked.

"Never have I ever," he said and he flashed me a wicked grin as he took his first sip.

"There is a chance I may be working with her again soon," I said, trying my best to sound casual. "We've been approached by a guy named Sebastian Detlefsen. You ever hear of him?"

He took a longer pull on his drink.

"I guess he's this rich tech guy who likes to hire soap actors to do scenes from their shows. It's good money."

Sly took another sip from his cup and then slung his gym bag over his shoulder. "It was great seeing you," he said with a friendly smile. "Say hi to Jasmine if you see her." Then he exited into the street.

CHAPTER TWENTY-ONE
NOW

ON THE SUBWAY my phone began buzzing in my pocket. I reached for it. Without my reading glasses, I could make out Corey's name. I hit ignore and continued to ride along, lost in thought. The car was half-empty. I watched a mother lean closer to a stroller to spoon food into her toddler's mouth and a man slumber nearby with earphones blocking out sound.

The wheels screeched to a halt and I exited at 86th Street. It was just a few blocks to my apartment. There was a slight nip in the air that hinted at turning leaves. Edgar was on duty as I entered the building so I stopped for a moment to chat with him. He was flipping though a copy of *The Daily News*.

"How are the boys?" I asked. I had finally sorted their names out: Nicholas and Anthony were seven.

"Growing like weeds," he said, closing the tabloid.

"Excited for Halloween?"

"Tons. They both want to be policemen this year, just like their old man."

I had recently learned that Edgar was ex-NYPD. One of the other doormen had told me.

"I miss that age," I said as he got up and hit the elevator button.

When I got back to the unit, I poured myself a glass of water and went to the living room. Traffic streamed by on Park. There was movement in my foyer, too, and I reflexively jumped.

"Sorry," Corey said, "I guess I didn't hear you when you came in." He had emerged from Riley's bedroom holding his phone and wallet. "What's up, my friend? Long time."

"Just busy with the stage shows," I said.

"Should I be insulted that I haven't been invited?" he asked me.

"I'm not sure I can get anyone in. It's a very tight guest list."

"No, I mean by this dude. He's asked you and Jasmine to do it. Where do I fit into this?"

Now was not the time to point out that Ford had also been asked to do it. Catharine had even driven to Ithaca to pitch the idea to him. But Corey's character, Olli, was less central to the plotting. He was the local police detective often brought in to investigate other people's stories. It was entirely possible he just wasn't important enough to generate interest in a show.

"Hey, I've got some news," Corey said. "I tried to call you a earlier but you didn't pick up. The woman subletting my apartment found a place and wants to move out on the first. I should be out of your hair in a few days."

"You're not in my hair," I said, meaning it. I had enjoyed having him.

I wondered if there would ever be a comfortable time to bring up what I had seen on the zip drive. I recalled plotlines on the show, when characters went through months of misunderstandings because no one had the guts to address each other directly. Was I as bad as Mira?

"I've got something I need to give back to you," he said, wandering back to Riley's room. He emerged with a yellow chapbook. "Hope you don't mind. I saw it and was sucked in. Did you read this?"

I still hadn't read more than one of the poems in Esther's collection. It had been sitting with all my research on the dining room table.

"It's weird. The poems are all about this girl who was molested by her uncle, who is this fire and brimstone preacher. She then ends up deeply depressed in a motel room looking at a Jesus prayer card that has been stuck into the Gideon bible. It gives her enough hope to survive."

That last bit I had read. The final poem was called "*Jesus at Motel 6.*"

I took the chapbook from Corey. I would definitely read it more closely. I still wasn't sure what this had to do with Ian's death but it might offer some clues. I wondered if this was Esther's story thinly veiled. Had she gone off the rails after what Ian and I did to her?

"It's amazing what people can survive, isn't it?" Corey said. "Humans are pretty durable."

Or were they? Ian's death showed the limits to endurance. Some people snap and either turn on themselves or others. It probably happened more often than I realized.

"You're certainly a survivor, Corey. I can't imagine being cast out by my mother the way you were. I'm so sorry that happened to you. It's pure evil what she did to you."

I had never been quite so forthright with Corey. The expression on his face was inscrutable. Maybe shame, maybe gratification.

"Not that my mother is perfect," I said. "I bear the mark of parental indifference."

"You've never said so," he said. I sensed his hunger to know that he was not alone.

"I have called her every Sunday since Riley was born. I think if I didn't she might forget about me for months at a time. Motherhood was something she did for eighteen years. It's like she graduated from me when I left home."

I felt awkward revealing this, wondering if there were any part of him that judged me for this. What did it say about me that my mother wasn't interested in me? At least he could blame homophobia for his situation. I had no one to blame but myself.

I left Corey standing in my living room, the revelation hanging in the air. He could take from it what he wanted.

When my phone rang a short time later, I answered without looking.

"Maggie, it's Sly."

"Hello again." I was doing my best acting to disguise my surprise that I was hearing from him.

"After I saw you this morning, I felt bad about leaving so abruptly so I called Jasmine and she gave me your number. I hope it's alright that I'm calling."

"Of course," I said.

"I'm wondering if maybe we can talk. I'd prefer to do it in person. Are you still staying with your son?"

Oh, dear. That lie. I had almost forgotten about it.

"Yes," I said.

"Well, I live at 14 Washington Square West. Do you know it?"

After four days surveilling his building from the park, I kind of did feel that I knew it.

"Why don't you meet me here tomorrow at 10? I'm on the fourteenth floor. 14D."

I hung up the phone. This was turning out to be an eventful day.

After my routine this week, it almost felt old hat to approach Sly's building. It was a utilitarian structure with a distinct academic feel. You could imagine that this had once been student or faculty housing. There was no doorman, so after Sly buzzed me in, I took the elevator to his floor.

"Welcome to my abode," he said as he ushered me in. The apartment was a large rectangle with hardwood floors and a sliding glass door opening onto a terrace. The walls were painted avocado green.

"Great view," I said, casting a glance at the park and the skyline beyond.

"Can I offer you something? I usually get my coffee out, but I do have tea."

"I'm fine, thanks," I said. I wondered why Kenzie couldn't visit him here. He appeared to live alone.

"So I was a little freaked out by your question yesterday," he said, gesturing for me to take a seat on his couch. I took a spot facing the fireplace.

"I hope I didn't cross a line. I was just curious about your experiences."

"You were approached by Sebastian Detlefsen?"

"By his assistant, Catharine Nash."

Sly chuckled. "Oh, I had forgotten about her. That was pretty slick of him. Hire a hot girl to woo people in."

"I did a party for him a while back," I said. "There was a set that was identical to Mira's bedroom. They hired a couple of actors to play the other characters in the scene. It all seemed on the up and up."

"At first mine did too. This guy isn't an idiot. There is a grooming period."

"Although something strange did happen. I don't know what to make of it. That's why I wanted to talk to you."

"You got a weird note."

I felt the blood drain from my face. "Yes."

"And it was about someone you care about."

"Well, not exactly. It was almost like it was a note from beyond."

Sly shook his head. He was making irregular eye contact, focusing more on his large hands. He had a silver thumb ring on one. He got up and walked over to a wall. There were three oil paintings. He summoned me over.

I got up and settled my gaze on the one he was pointing to. It was a painting of a boy, about seven. He was sitting on the stoop of a brownstone, a red ball on the step below.

"This is my little brother, Elliot. He's sitting on the stairs to my grandparents' house in Harlem."

"It's a nice piece," I said. It reminded me a little bit of the works I had seen in the Eight Ball bar that first day I met Catharine.

"Thank you," he said. "My dad painted it. He was an artist. This was his apartment originally. He was a visiting artist at NYU."

I waited, not quite sure what was coming next.

"As you may know, *All My Children* went off the air about four years ago. At first I was glad to be out of the grind, those endless days waiting on set. But after about a year, I was bored. I was taking an acting class and working with some friends on a play. One night after rehearsal, I found a business card stuck under my wipers."

"The infinity circle," I said. "Looks like a figure eight on its side."

"That's the one," Sly said. "I tossed it and didn't think twice about it. But about a week later I got another one. This one was slid under my door here. I got curious so I called. And then I met Catharine at that same coffee house where we ran into each other yesterday. She seemed nice enough. They were offering easy money."

I had a sinking feeling that I knew what was coming next.

"So I did the party. They had created a set that resembled Lucky's office at the nightclub. There was a popular episode where he got shot sitting at his desk. They hired an actress to play the woman who shot me; the original actress had died."

"Where was the party?" I asked.

"Some warehouse in Williamsburg," Sly said. He walked back over the couch and I joined him. "My car got stolen that night but that's another story. Anyway, as I was waiting on set, I opened the desk drawer. I was just curious. The stuff inside the drawers was authentic. They had mocked up billing documents and matchbooks with the nightclub's name. They even had an address in Pine Valley."

"They did the same for me," I said. "They hired one of our set designers to recreate the Wilder guesthouse. It was like being back at the studio."

"And along with that stuff in the desk drawer, there was a note. It was written in crayon. Red crayon. I'll never forget it. It said, *Sly Sly Can you help me? I'm out where the apples grow.*"

I sat in silence until he said, "My little brother died when he was seven. He drowned at an apple orchard."

My eyes moistened as I considered this. What kind of twisted person would do this to a man who had experienced such a loss? At least my note had been from Jacoby. It was in character.

"That's horrible, Sly. I don't know how anyone could be so cruel. I'm so sorry."

He left the room for a bit and returned with a glass of water. He took a sip.

"I just want to warn you. Sebastian Detlefsen is a sick fuck. I wouldn't want anyone to go through what he did to me."

"I did receive a note, Sly. It was written to Mira from Jacoby in the back of one of her journals on set. I'm not suggesting it's as bad as what happened to you, but I did care about Ian. He died recently. It's why I wanted to talk to you."

Sly shook his head. He was a huge guy, blocking most of the door to the hallway behind him.

"And it's why I was willing to talk to you. I wanted to warn you. This is just the first step."

"What do you mean, first step?" I was processing his words a little slower than normal.

"They're going to come after you again, Maggie. The second step is even more convincing. They'll keep doing it until you believe. I did and it nearly destroyed me."

"What did they get you to believe?" I asked.

Sly fixed me with a steely look. I felt a bit unnerved, almost afraid. "They made me think that Elliot was still alive."

"How?"

"This young kid—he was maybe eighteen - started turning up everywhere: my gym, my favorite grocery store, my coffee shop. Finally he approached me. He said that for many years his family believed he had died when he was seven. He had been kidnapped as a kid by a cult and they faked his death. He invited me to a support group for other abductees and to a website where there were testimonials from doctors and other professionals who claimed to be in on it. There was a testimonial from a funeral director who claimed he told parents to choose cremation because the trauma of seeing their dead child would be too great. Of course I didn't believe him at first. It sounded like some stupid soap plot. But he was so earnest that his story just seemed plausible. I was this close to believing them. I never figured out what Sebastian was up to, but I just feel it is my moral imperative to warn you. This is not going to end well."

"Thank you for telling me," I said. I was feeling slightly embarrassed that I had so naively gotten involved with this.

Sly and I talked for a bit more – about our work, about mutual acquaintances – and then I headed out.

CHAPTER TWENTY-TWO
NOW

I FOUND MYSELF on the street outside of Sly's apartment, not quite sure how I got there. I was completely parched, my throat dry. I began walking north without any thought to stopping for a bottle of water. My mind was swimming with the story he had just told me, about what Sebastian Detlefsen had done to him after he had found that first note.

I stepped onto the sidewalk, a siren wailing as an ambulance careened down the street a block away. Finally, near St. Vincent's Hospital, I found a bodega and went inside. A young Korean man was talking animatedly on his blue tooth. I grabbed a bottle of Fuji Water and paid with my card, barely interacting with him. I uncapped it and drank it down, the soft cold slipping down. I finished the bottle and tossed it into a recycling bin before exiting back onto Seventh Avenue.

How could Catharine Nash be complicit in this? Surely she couldn't be involved to the degree that she was without knowing what was happening. I thought of our interactions, of her casual sincerity that drew me in. I had never thought to Google her, to find out what her life was like outside her job. I imagined her spending her summers in the Hamptons, building sandcastles with her nephews and sneaking out to a clambake with college friends. What would possess such a person to play mind games with someone she hardly knew?

I pulled out my phone and dialed a number. He picked up right away.

"I was just thinking about you," he said, which I knew was a lie. Ford Sather did not seem like a man who spent many idle thoughts on women.

"I had a favor to ask you," I said. "How long have you lived in Ithaca?"

"I moved here about five years ago," he said. "Why?"

"I was wondering if I could pick your brain about the area. There is only so much you can glean from online research."

"You planning to move up this way or something? Real estate is reasonable."

"You know what, I'm about to go down into the subway. Can we talk later?"

"My vegetable garden is blooming. You up for a road trip?"

I wasn't sure what Ford had in mind beyond dinner and some local history.

"Are you thinking tonight?" I said. I didn't want to seem too eager.

"That would work."

"I've got something but I can reschedule," I said, a blatant lie. "Can I bring you something from the city?"

Ford's house was a white Victorian with box windows, a slanted roof, and a front garden full of flowers. When I pulled up and parked, he was sitting on a porch swing, drinking a mug of coffee. He had a thick paperback with a cracked spine sitting next to him.

"What are you reading?" I asked, feeling shy. In some ways, I hardly knew this guy.

"It's a novel set in Madrid during the Franco years. Did you know that he outlawed handholding in public? The protagonists are a young couple who are secretly attending a co-ed school. The boys and girls all line up and go into different buildings. The state doesn't know that they're mixing with each other inside. I think something tragic is about to happen."

"Sounds like a good story," I said. "I hope I'm not interrupting anything."

"I've been so busy reading I haven't even thought about dinner. I've got plenty of vegetables in the garden. How do you feel about an herb omelet and fried potatoes? Salad? I got some bread at the Farmer's Market this morning."

"I'm an actress, Ford. I'm always hungry." And I always tried to avoid saturated fat. I decided I could take a night off.

He got up and opened the screen door for me. His interior was sanded wood floors, Shaker furniture, and a white brick fireplace. There was a framed black and white photograph on the mantle above it.

"Your parents?" I said, casting a glance.

"Actually, that's my uncle, my dad's brother, with my mom. I love that photo of them. He raised me after she died."

"Where did you grow up?" It occurred to me that I knew almost nothing about the man I was dining with. Maybe once I had, but the detail had faded.

"New Haven mostly."

"He raised you as a single man?"

"He did. He always told me that there was order in art but not in life. Neither of us ever would have planned for the hand we were dealt and yet it worked out fairly well. He was a much better parent than my mother was. And my biological dad was a prick. His brother was polar opposite, though. Just an amazing guy."

"I never met my father," I said. I was surprised at how easy it was to talk to him. Peter and I had rarely talked this way. "I have never once missed him. Never wished he would come looking for me. At a certain point it just doesn't matter anymore."

"The power of myths is astonishing," Ford said. "This idea that everyone has a hole in their heart without a father. I never found that to be the case. In a lot of ways, I was better off without him."

We had walked back through the living room to a small gray kitchen. There was a Wedgewood stove, glass cupboards, and Formica flooring.

"There is a jar of iced tea in the fridge. Help yourself." Ford left through a screened back porch and was gone for a while. When he returned, he had a colander full of potatoes, carrots, and a few sprigs of rosemary.

"You got chickens back there, too?" I said, swilling my iced tea. It was sugarless, just the way I liked it.

"I rely on the Farmers' Market for that."

I washed and peeled the carrots and potatoes while Ford cracked eggs and chopped rosemary. We talked about theater – Harold Pinter, Tom Stoppard, Edward Albee – and then sat down and ate. The food was so good I could hardly clear my mouth to make conversation.

"Your uncle taught theater?" I asked.

"Yes. Yale Drama School. He taught me everything I know. He told me that actors need three things: a well-trained voice, a range of emotions, and an expressive physical body. He said that the worst actors are only focused on themselves. And the quote he used so often was, 'Acting is the ability to live truthfully under imaginary circumstances.'"

I think I had heard that said somewhere less artfully. I thought of how often those lines are crossed, and the imaginary connections begin to feel like truth. Is this what had caused me to feel enduring love for Ian, whom I barely knew? The imaginary felt real.

"I was so bad at not giving into it," I said, spearing a carrot with my fork. "I think most of my relationship with Ian was tied to that connection I felt in front of the camera. When we were alone it just felt like an extension of a script."

"You weren't the only one," he said. "Lines blurred plenty."

"You?" I said.

"I never did," he said. "I think I was too lost in Duncan's pathology to form that sort of social bond. But Ty was always pining for his co-stars."

A random fact slipped into my mind: Ty and Ford had met at Yale Drama School. They were friends even before the show. In fact, one of them had probably gotten the other the audition. They may have even been roommates our first season. It's funny how the mind forgets but then remembers.

"I never picked up on that," I said.

Ford laughed, taking a piece of bread. "Maggie, are you telling me you didn't notice what was going on between Ty and Jasmine?" He laughed good-naturedly as he slathered butter on the bread.

"They played siblings. It didn't occur to me."

"Cleopatra married her brother," Ford said. "It happens."

I cast my mind back on those days. During Riley's first year I was sleep-deprived. I often spent my breaks napping in my dressing room.

"Did this happen when she was married to Ian?" I was trying to do the mental math.

"They were both married," Ford said. "Le Scandal. I think it's why Ian and Jasmine divorced so quickly." It was the one blessing: their union was short-lived. By the time Riley was out of diapers, Ian was a single man again.

Scattered memories from the set crossed my mind like clouds across a summer sky. Ty, Jasmine, and me sitting on the set that was the Wilder breakfast room, the crew milling about to add color and heat to the food we were pretending to eat. I had never picked up on more than a collegial vibe between them. Was I really this clueless? It occurred to me that Ty hadn't shown up to Jasmine's dinner party. Maybe there was bad blood between them still.

"I wanted to ask you something," I said, shifting the focus. "Do you know anything about a local commune called Concordia?"

"Sure," Ford said. "The former leader owns a bookstore here in town with her son."

"What was your impression of it?"

"I don't know that I've ever actually been to the place, but it sounded pretty cool. Tamberlain was a seminary student who wanted to challenge the basic myth of the fall. They had a special liturgy that challenged the idea that Eve was sinful. Then they got shut down."

"Any idea why?"

"I think it was racist. The locals were suspicious of a black woman running a countercultural community. They shut it down but I'm not sure it was fair. She got sent away for a while for things white people do all the time."

"You know Tamberlain?"

"I wouldn't say that. I shop at her store from time to time. In fact, that book I was reading earlier was from there. Her son recommended it."

"The store is co-owned by a woman who once interned for the show. Esther Oden, do you remember her?"

Ford raised an eyebrow. "What are you suggesting about me and interns?"

I laughed good-naturedly, and then shifted the conversation.

"Did you ever follow up with Catharine Nash after that meeting you had with her? You said she drove up here to talk to you, right?"

He stared out the window and into the yard. "Yes, she did, but we just had that one conversation."

"You didn't Google her or anything?"

"It's not my practice, Maggie." It occurred to me I hadn't seen any sign of technology in his house. There was no TV, no computer, maybe not even a cell phone. He settled his gaze back on me. "Is something the matter?"

I felt a flood of words tumbling out just then: about the show I had done for Sebastian Detlefsen, the note I had found, the conversation with Jasmine, the meeting with Sly.

"There are a lot of sick people in this world, Maggie," he said finally. "It's best to be cautious."

"I didn't get a bad vibe from her, though, did you?" I asked.

"What can you know of a person in twenty minutes?" Ford asked, getting up from the table.

We cleared away dinner, leaving the dishes to soak, and went upstairs. A cool breeze moved through the hallway from opened windows. When we reached his bedroom, he turned me around and pulled me to him. He kissed me deeply, his tongue flicking in and out of my mouth. I felt myself go a bit weak, longing for more.

We stood there in the doorway, lost in the kiss, and then I led him to the bed. I stripped off his clothes and mine along with them, straddling him as we lay back on the bed. I moved up and down on him, feeling the light breeze curl around me and touch my neck. When we were finished, I pulled myself off and fell onto the bed next to him. I fell into a light, content sleep.

When I awoke the next morning, the house was empty. I pulled on my clothes, running my fingers through my hair as I walked down the stairs. I thought about leaving Ford a note and then reconsidered it. I left his house, found my car, and headed off.

CHAPTER TWENTY-THREE
THEN

A WOMAN WITH a commanding halo of hair got up in front of the chapel, holding a fresh apple in her hand. "We know why we are here," she said, holding the fruit aloft. Striped pink, supple and ready for harvest. "Thousands of years ago, in a place far more beautiful than this one, an act of evil, of defiance, happened. People rebelled against the true spirit of God and fell into the wages of sin of death."

Around the chapel, voices began to rise in affirmation. A woman, resplendent in red silk, raised her arms in the air, swaying from side to side. Her hair was a wild bush of red, aflame.

"And our beloved sisters pay the price for this sin," she said. "We have been told a very poisonous story and many of us have believed it." She closed her hands around the apple, bowing her head.

"We worship her!" A voice called out. "Now and always."

The audience swayed in time, calling out, until Tamberlain spoke again.

"The evildoers are at the gates, but we will continue to walk the straight path. We honor Eve and her sacrifice."

She walked to a simple stone altar. Murmuring prayers she knew by rote, she pulled out a switchblade and cut the apple. She sliced until there were enough for everyone. An acolyte stood next to her, pouring fresh cider into a silver chalice.

She walked forward to the lip of the aisle. The congregants lined up two by two, moving slowly in time to a drum.

"Sister Johanna, do you affirm the innocence of Eve and reject the patriarch who defamed her?"

"I do," the woman replied, taking a sliver of apple on her tongue and washing it down with cider. She closed her hands in prayer, pausing for a moment, and then moved aside. Another woman took the place left empty by her departure. "Sister Isidora, do you affirm the innocence of Eve and reject the patriarch who defamed her?"

"I do," the woman replied and took a bit of the apple.

Someone stepped into the spot she had vacated. Tamberlain looked down at her with kind eyes. "Sister Stranger, do you affirm the innocence of Eve and reject the patriarch who defamed her?"

She took the apple and placed it on the stranger's tongue. It was tart and crisp. "I do," the woman said.

After communion was over, the crowd sat in silence. After a few moments, a woman in purple talked about imagery of women in the media. After a few more silent moments, another woman spoke about a recent honor killing in India that had made the news. Tamberlain sat in front of the stone altar in a cross-legged position, listening intently to their stories.

After a lull that felt like it might be the last, the guest rose. She had a twig-like figure and her voice was barely above a whisper. "Thank you for welcoming us today. My daughter and I are here to heal from an evil man. He does bad things to women."

Tamberlain returned from her pillow to the stone altar. After a period of silence, she said. "We hear your stories, we honor your struggles. Blessed be to Eve."

CHAPTER TWENTY-FOUR

NOW

I HIT THE highway, lost in thought, heading unthinkingly to my destination. I was remembering one afternoon at Ian's cottage, after we had been sleeping together a few months. I had felt a sudden wave of nausea that caused me to jump out of bed and run into the bathroom. I turned on the overhead fan, hoping to drown out the sound of my retching, pulling my hair back as I vomited. I knew in an instant that I was pregnant.

I had been pregnant once before. My high school boyfriend Graham and I had been careless, not using a condom one freezing afternoon in January of my senior year. When I got the test results, I had told him, and then I told my mother, and together we drove to Health Services on campus for an abortion. A few months later, I graduated and went to New York.

One thing I knew for sure that afternoon, standing in Ian's bathroom, my wan face staring back at me in his mirror: this pregnancy would end differently.

❧

I could see the city's jagged outline in the foreground as I continued to drive in silence. When my phone rang, I hit speaker.

"Mom, it's Riley," he said. He often began a phone call this way. It always made me chuckle.

"Thanks for clearing that up," I said. I was surprised when I didn't hear a muffled laugh in response. This was one of our standard routines.

"Mom, I'm at the hospital with dad. He's had an accident."

My heart accelerated. "What happened? Is he OK?"

"Mom, I don't know much. I got a call from an EMT because I am his emergency contact in his phone. He was brought in an ambulance from somewhere. They aren't telling me anything."

Peter traveled a lot to keep up with his clients. He could have been anywhere.

"Sweetie, just hold on. I will be there as soon as I can. Which hospital are you at?"

My son was crying. "Mom, I can't remember the name. I have to ask someone."

"Baby, it's OK," I said, tears stinging my eyes. My foot hit the accelerator. "Just ask someone where you are and I will be there as soon as I can."

When he got back on the phone and told me the hospital name, I had heard of it.

I had visited there once when a co-star on the show had a baby.

It took me another hour to get to Midtown. I found my way to the hospital parking lot. It was nearly full. There was a set of orange elevators near a ticket machine. I rode to the floor number Riley had given me. When the doors parted with a ding, I was hit by the preternatural silence. An attending nurse was typing with his back turned as I entered the foyer. In a waiting room to the right, I saw my son slumped on a vinyl couch.

"The doctor was just here," Riley said, instantly calming me with his new demeanor. I hugged him and held him for a moment too long. "Dad was hiking with a client and he fell off a trail. He's going to be fine."

I exhaled and began crying. I had felt suspended in motion since the first call had come. What a relief to have some facts to hold onto.

"Any idea where this happened?" I said.

"I think Breakneck Ridge was the name," Riley said. "They said he lost his footing and fell about fifty feet."

I ran my hands through my son's hair, remembering him at two and five and seven. Where was my little boy? He stood nearly a foot over his mother these days.

The elevator dinged again. Veronica appeared with two plastic bags. I averted my eyes when Riley leaned down to kiss her.

"I thought you might like some food," she said. "I wasn't sure what to get so there's Cuban and Chinese."

I dug in greedily, opening a carton of beef lo mein and another of Kung pao chicken. I was so hungry that I tore open a fortune cookie and ate it while the entrees cooled.

We were soon all chowing down in companionable silence, chatting in lulls, casting glances at a muted TV that showed the news headlines in a repetitive loop.

I was stringing my last lo mein noodle on my plastic fork when a woman in scrubs appeared.

"I'm Doctor Pera," she said, officiously offering a hand. I dropped the fork and shook it. "Your husband took a pretty bad fall. He has broken his left leg in two places. He also broke a rib that nearly pierced his lung. He was very lucky. If he had fallen a little farther, he might have died."

I exhaled with gratitude. "Can we see him?"

"I'm afraid not. He is heavily sedated. I would suggest coming back tomorrow during visiting hours."

"How about the person he was with?"

She consulted with her clipboard. "Right. She was treated for minor injuries and released. She was only harmed trying to help him. She didn't take a fall herself."

"What was her name?"

The doctor lifted eyeglasses from a chain around her neck and put them on. "I can't release a patient's name," the doctor said, writing something on her clipboard.

"So I guess we can come back tomorrow," I said after Doctor Pera left. "Why don't you call me when you plan to head over? It would be nice to visit your father together."

Veronica gathered up the food packaging and went to find a garbage.

"Mom, I know who Dad was with."

I looked at him imploringly.

"Her name is Abby. I've met her. She said I used to know her son."

Abby Harper was in my moms' group when our boys were little. She was a graphic artist married to a lawyer. I hadn't thought of her in years.

"Do you remember Henry Harper?" I asked my son. "You were best friends in elementary school."

Riley shrugged. "Maybe."

It was amazing what kids forgot. Riley and Henry were two peas for most of their childhood. They had even visited my mother together several times. When Henry's parents had gotten divorced, he moved downtown and switched schools. Now it appeared that his mother was dating Peter. They had gone hiking on the weekend. This was so not like my husband, not since the days we first met and couldn't stand to be apart.

I couldn't sleep that night. After tossing and turning until my clock read 5:03, I decided to get up and stay focused. I rooted around the kitchen and pulled together a gift package for Peter: a Toblerone, a box of crackers, a bag of salted nuts. I pulled a few books off his office shelves and wrapped a blanket in with everything. Since the last time he was here, I hadn't been back to storage to find his yearbooks. I got dressed and grabbed a flashlight.

The service elevator was positively creepy at this time of night. When it stopped on the fourth floor, I imagined a straggly haired stranger coming at me with a knife. I pushed the fear out of my mind and focused on my task at hand. When the elevator doors parted, I was in a large open space with thirty mesh cages. I made a beeline for 11B and unlocked it. There seemed to be fewer boxes than the last time I was here. Peter had taken the kayak and all the camping equipment. I opened one box to find Christmas lights on top, another to find Ziploc bags full of black and white photographs. Towards the back, under a tarp, there were half a dozen smaller cartons. I used an Exacto knife to slice into them and root around.

There was a mandala from a play I had done one year, a pile of Riley's Halloween costumes, and a bunch of old photography equipment. After going through every box, I had found nothing. I leaned on the mesh wall, feeling slightly woozy from the work. Then a thought occurred to me: the yearbooks would likely be with stuff from his mother. I reopened the box with the Ziploc bags of black and white photos and took them out. There were stacks and stacks of family photos. At the bottom there were four yearbooks and a bag full of paper report cards.

Victorious, I grabbed the two from Cornell and went about the task of closing up all the containers I had just opened. The overhead light flashed off and then on, a flicker that felt like a signal. A hulking body came towards me from the elevator, his footsteps heavy against the cement floor.

"Miss Grayson, do you ever sleep?"

It was Edgar. He was in his street clothes, a pair of jeans, boots, and a NYPD hoodie. He was holding a to-go tray with four cups of coffee and a brown bag.

"You want black or white?" He asked, proffering the cups. "The blacks are in front."

I took one from the back and had a hearty sip. Warm, syrupy liquid spilled down my throat. It was in an Acropolis cup.

"Got bagels and schmear, too," he said. "Wanna come have breakfast with me? My shift is over in a few hours. I'm just taking my break."

Something about the moment made me say yes. We walked back out and through a dingy hallway. Edgar removed his ring of keys and opened a brown door similar to the one that fronted my kitchen. Inside there was a small unit with a couch, a TV, a kitchenette and a bathroom. There was a standing rack with doormen coats. There was also a small surveillance monitor that showed the front desk.

"Wow, it's like a dressing room for doormen," I said and then flushed at the comment. I hoped I didn't sound classist. I had just never seen the inner workings of the building.

"You really think I take my break in that coat?" He said with a guffaw. He rustled into the paper bag and pulled out a few bagels. There was a tub of whipped cream cheese as well. He ripped a sesame bagel in half and ate it in a few hearty bites. "So what were you looking for at five in the morning?"

"Peter asked me to find his yearbooks from college."

"That's dedication. I haven't seen him around much. How's he doing?"

"He's been busy," I said. Edgar seemed like the kind of traditional, macho guy who might judge a woman for being separated. If I told him about the hospital stay, it would just cause more confusion when Peter didn't come back.

I took half a poppy seed bagel and spread a thin layer of schmear on it. I took a bite.

"You can just feel autumn in the air this morning," Edgar said. "Mornings this time of year are my favorite thing. I love being out on the streets at this time."

I smiled. "Do you do any moonlighting? Side gigs?"

"Sometimes," he said, draining his blue Acropolis cup and opening the lid to another one. "What do you have in mind?"

"I'm doing a little research for a play. I need to find out about a woman who was arrested. Do you still have access to police records?"

He grinned at me. He had visible cream cheese on his upper lip. "I can get them, sure."

"What is your rate?"

He shrugged. "Eighty an hour, plus expenses."

"I'll double that if you can get it done quickly. The woman's name is Johanna Ray. She is incarcerated upstate at the Finger Lakes Correctional Institute. I have to find out the name of the minor involved in the case."

"Let me write this down," Edgar said, rooting around in a closet until he found a notebook and pen.

"Also if you can run a records check on Corey Broderick. See if has any kind of criminal history."

"Wasn't that the guy who was staying with you?"

Great. So Corey had probably chatted him up. "Yes. I think he stole something from me."

"Bastard," Edgar said.

When I woke, I had no idea what time it was. I swiped my hand across my nightstand but found that my phone wasn't there. I pulled myself up and padded through my foyer. I found the two yearbooks stacked on the table with my phone on top. I swiped. There were three texts from Riley, starting at 7 am, each about ten minutes apart.

Morning, mom. You up?

Planning to head over soon. You up?

V and I are going to get breakfast first.

My clock read 11:11. I swiped and dialed, waiting for Riley to answer.

"Hey sleepyhead," my son said, "We decided to go ahead of you when you didn't get back to us."

"Sorry, hon, it's been a kind of weird few days. You there with dad now?"

"Yup, do you want to talk to him?"

Before I had a chance to answer, he passed the phone to his father.

"Maggie, hi," Peter sounded groggy but otherwise much as I remembered him.

"I'm so glad to hear your voice," I said. "How are you feeling?"

"Well, I'll never play the piano again."

I laughed out loud. This was an old joke between us. He could only be in his right mind to use it.

"I'm headed out now," I said. "I've got a few things for you."

"Listen, Mags, there is no reason you need to come over. Riley and Veronica are here with me, and Abby will be over in a bit."

The name stung a bit. "Abby Harper, Henry's mother?"

"Yes, she was with me on the hike on Saturday. Thank goodness or who knows where I would be today."

"You're socializing with her?"

"We're dating, Maggie. I'm sorry you had to find out this way."

"No worries," I said. "I'm seeing someone too. Doesn't mean I can't visit my ex in the hospital."

His next words were cold. "Maggie, at this point I think a visit might be more of an inconvenience. I've had barely a moment to myself since I woke up."

Here he was again: the man I fell out of love with. I hung up with a curt goodbye.

CHAPTER TWENTY-FIVE
THEN

Late in the summer of Esther, as I had come to think of it, Page invited me on a weekend trip to Nantucket. One of her co-workers had a family house there and a group of his friends were meeting for one last clambake before it got colder. In mid-September, a whole group of us flew up in a tiny prop plane owned by the guy's family. It was so small and rickety I thought I could feel myself falling through the sky as we flew.

The house was enormous, right on the beach, and we spent days smoking weed and boiling lobsters. Couples paired off: Page with a co-worker, other women and men, until only Peter and I were left. On our last day we were divided into teams and sent out to the beach to build sandcastles. Page had put Peter and me together, thinking our sensibilities might mesh, and she was right. We commandeered an impressive Empire State Building and won the competition. For years, I had a picture of us that day framed and in our living room. I was leaning on Peter and he was tilting his head down towards my small body. Our sandcastle was behind us. We looked like a couple about to fall in love.

Flying home in the rickety plane, Peter reached over and held my hand as we descended onto a lighted landing strip on Long Island. On the tarmac, as we all piled into taxis and said our goodbyes, he promised to call me. A few weeks later, he did.

What Peter didn't know about me, when we met that giddy weekend in Nantucket, was that a few months before I had gotten pregnant by Ian. A drug store test had confirmed what I had known in my gut that day in Ian's bathroom. I was sick for a week, sleeping on cold bathroom tiles to be near the toilet, making my way to the kitchen for saltines and ginger ale every few hours.

When the illness passed, I was also happy. Although I was young, it felt right. I thought of my mother waking up to bloody sheets in her U Mass dorm room, walking down the hall to vomit in porcelain. If she could swing single motherhood, so could I.

I waited a few weeks to tell Ian. It was hard to keep it from him, since he had an insatiable drive and was after me nearly every day on the set, dipping into my dressing room on breaks or resting his thick fingers on my backside between takes. I tried to pass my queasiness off as seasonal flu. One night, when the worst of the nausea had passed, I told him. We had just gone upstairs after watching a movie in his screening room. He was leaning into the refrigerator, pulling out two bottles of beer, when I blurted it out.

For a moment, I thought he hadn't heard me. Then he shut the fridge with some force. "That can never happen," he said turning around to meet my gaze. He spoke with a coldness I had never experienced from him.

"It has happened. I didn't plan it," I said. I reflexively put my hands on my belly, wanting to protect our baby.

"Well, it needs to not happen," he said. "I will not be a father."

He said it with such resolute swiftness that I couldn't release a reply.

I was fortunate, I suppose. A few weeks later, I woke up in my apartment on 13th Street in a puddle of blood. Nature had erased our mistake. I called in sick and cried all day, never telling Ian how the pregnancy ended. I couldn't bear to see relief, satisfaction even, cross his face when he heard the news.

There is an episode of *Wild Hearts* from that day. It was the only taping in fifteen seasons that I missed. They hired an attractive blonde flight attendant who had done extra work for us to play Mira for one day. I knew the actress vaguely; we sometimes chatted in the make up trailer or while getting coffee from craft services. She was a sweet woman from

Savannah who had yet to be eaten alive by show business. The episode was set during the harvest crush at the vineyard. Mira and Jacoby were in love by then, but she was just about to learn that he had lied about his past.

I watched the episode once, many years later, on YouTube. The flight attendant did a decent job embodying the character. She flubbed a few lines, but who could blame her? She had been called in on a moment's notice. What struck me more, though, was Ian's performance. Watching him that day, staring into her eyes with the same intense, steely gaze and earnest tenderness that I played opposite, it was as if I had never existed. It made no difference to him who was standing in front of him. We were all exactly the same.

CHAPTER TWENTY-SIX
NOW

When I heard a rap on the door, I was confused. I sat up, still lost in sleep, and a blanket dropped to the floor. I was in my living room. Outside it was getting dark. Some of my neighbors in the building opposite had snapped on their lights. I had slept the whole day. The last thing I remembered was paging through Peter's yearbook in the foyer after our phone call ended. When I padded through, I saw that I had left one open. I shut it and looked through the peephole. A distorted, funhouse image appeared.

"I told you I was fast," Edgar said after I opened the door. He was out of his doorman coat. He must have stayed in the neighborhood after his shift ended. "I got that information you requested."

I ushered him in and kicked the dimmer lights up a notch. There were lilies wilting in a vase on the table that needed to be replaced.

"So Johanna Ray went away for statutory rape in 1989," he said, reading from a flip notebook. I wondered if he always carried one around with him. "She was given a seven-year sentence. They boy in question was sixteen at the time of the events, seventeen by the time she went away. His name was Sidney Calkins. From what I could gather, he was a foster kid who lived in Ithaca. Not sure how the two met."

"So she was eligible for parole in what, 1996?" That was the year the show started. I wondered if she had had any contact with Ian during that time. He had certainly never given any indication of it.

"She got addicted to meth while on the inside," Hector said. "She was no sooner released then she got hit with a twenty-five year sentence for dealing."

"Any idea what happened to this kid?" I asked. "What was his name again?"

"Sidney Calkins. No idea. I could look into it if you like. Foster kids often become homeless, though. The paper trail might be a challenge."

"Please do," I said. "Listen, what do I owe you for today?"

We exchanged pleasantries while I pulled a few fifties out of a coffee can.

"Miss Grayson, may I ask why you want to play this woman?"

"Pardon me?" I said.

"You're going to play a woman who raped a boy? Why?"

I had almost forgotten my lie from earlier. I had told him needed the information about Johanna because I was doing research for a play. "It's my job to find the humanity in all people," I said.

Edgar shook his head. "Not me. My job was always to put those scumbags away. And these days it's to keep them out of your apartment."

"Who is on shift right now?" I asked.

"Solomon," he said. "You need something?"

"Just let him know I'm expecting a package. Amazon prime." I had ordered a copy of *Vertigo* during my sleepless night after I couldn't find a way to stream it.

"You got it."

"Oh, and anything on Corey Broderick?"

"I had my buddy run a records check. He is clean. Not even a speeding ticket."

I thanked him and closed the door after he left. He was a good man. I felt a little safer in the building knowing he was in charge.

Peter's yearbooks were still on the foyer table. I grabbed one and went to the living room couch, paging through it while I listened to some vinyl. There were chapters on academics, sports, campus life. This edition was Peter's senior year so I paged back to his photo. There he was on the top of a page: Peter Alexander Davis. Seeing him at this age, his shaggy curls and dark eyes unweathered by time and tide, I could recall the attraction I once felt for him.

I flipped to the next page, marveling at the lack of '80s hair. These folks knew to avoid hairspray even then. And the names, too: *Buffy Dalton, Xandra Dunne.* They were probably both partners in law firms these days.

My eyes fell on another name. *Sebastian Detlefsen.* I bugged out a bit, zeroing my focus on the photo. He had the same Nordic features but had a ponytail in his college days. I took a snap of his entry and texted it to Peter with a note.

Do you remember this guy? Psych major. Graduated your year at Cornell.

I waited a few minutes for a chime.

Yes, world-class asshole. There were rumors he had sex with his sister.

Now was not the time to tell my estranged husband that I had accepted cash payment from this guy in exchange four hours' work. I hoped it wouldn't come up at tax time.

Another chime: *why do you ask?*

Since I had no reasonable reply that was truthful, I let it lie. Peter would probably forget in a few days anyway.

A few days went by. I watched and re-watched *Vertigo.* It is the story of a San Francisco cop, Scottie Ferguson, who is on leave from his job after he bungles a case due to his fear of heights. An old friend hires Scotty to follow his wife during the day. He fears that his wife is mentally ill.

It occurred to me that Julian had borrowed heavily from noir on our show. I had never watched much of it so I didn't realize it at the time. Duncan Wilder was clearly influenced by Norman Bates in *Psycho* and I could see shades of Scottie Ferguson in Corey's character.

I sent Julian a Facebook message asking if she wanted to get together. I was nervous proposing it; she still felt very much like the boss. I was relieved when she replied with an invitation to have dinner at her place at the end of the week.

The night in question, I arrived early. The nerves began to hit when I stepped into the wide elevator and slowly moved up to her roof-top apartment.

She beckoned me inside with a wave of her hand. She was wearing a bowling shirt and Doc Martens.

"I just got back from running errands," she said. "So please hang out with me while I cook for you." On her countertops were four bags of groceries from Gristedes. She unpacked salmon fillets, Romano cheese, a bag of bowtie pasta. She uncorked a bottle of pinot grigio and served me a glass. I stood idly by while she opened boxes and put pans on her stovetop.

"Is Veruca staying with you?" I asked. The apartment seemed vacant except for us.

"On and off, yes," Julian said. "I have always had trouble keeping track of that one."

"So what was it you wanted to talk to me about?" she asked. There was a large pot of water beginning to boil. She measured out a cup of bowtie pasta.

"I recently learned that Ian's mother is incarcerated. Did you know anything about that?"

Julian grunted a bit. She was melting some butter in a saucepan. She opened a bag of flour. "I think Veruca mentioned it at some point."

"I've been wondering a bit about the Duncan plotline. I always really liked it. It reminded me a bit of a genderqueer take on Hitchcock. The way Duncan was always cross-dressing and he seemed obsessed with Mira's innocence. It reminds me of Norman Bates and Marion Crane."

"Not bad analysis," Julian said, whisking the flour into the melted butter. She ground a pepper mill over it and added a heaping stack of shredded Romano cheese. She stirred for a while and then removed it from the heat source.

"Do you remember what inspired the story?"

"I was inspired by a lot of classic movies. My parents weren't around a lot when I was growing up so I spent my summers watching soaps and going to the movies. There was this air-conditioned theater in the Bronx that showed suspense double features. I saw every Hitchcock movie there. I did always like Norman Bates. I think you may be onto something."

"It was kind of an edgy plot. Was the network OK with it?"

"It was a bit of a hard sell. No one was ready to see that kind of content back then. But they allowed it because I convinced them that Duncan was in a state of arrested development. That was how we came up with the idea to have those scenes in the attic, where he was making clothes for Mira. It was like she was his doll or something. It seemed less threatening to the audience that way."

Julian removed two thick salmon steaks from butcher's paper and put them in a frying pan. She poured me another glass of wine.

The door code buzzed and Veruca entered. Her hair was down today and she was wearing a Lolita dress. She gave me the standard sullen hello and began rooting around the grocery bags.

"Is that cream sauce?" she said, scrutinizing Julian's creation. "You know I don't eat butter." She pulled out a plastic box of prewashed salad and dumped it into a bowl. Then she covered it in red dressing and started chomping on it.

"Veruca, you said you saw Ian just a few months before he died, right?"

"My friend has a houseboat near Sea Cliff. I was staying with him for a while last summer to escape the city heat. I bumped into Ian occasionally. He had put on some weight, but other than that seemed pretty happy. Or maybe he put on weight because he was happy." She crunched on her spinach.

"And you said you saw him with Esther once or twice, right? At the breakfast place?"

"Yes, and then later in the summer I saw him with another woman. They were all lovey-dovey."

"What did she look like? The later one?"

"Attractive brunette, big tits. Kind of his type, I think."

So at some point Ian and Esther had broken up. Maybe she was angry about the new love.

Julian had set two plates at the dining room table. She was lighting candles. I left Veruca sitting on the counter with her half-eaten bowl of salad and took a place across from my old boss. I took a fork full of salmon and speared a few pieces of bowtie pasta. I put the food in my mouth. It tasted like heaven.

CHAPTER TWENTY-SEVEN
NOW

My taxi screeched to a halt in front of the building and I jumped out, waving the driver off with a twenty. Soloman was on duty for the night shift. After he hit the button to call the elevator, he pulled a thick manila envelope from behind the desk. "This was just delivered for you," he said. I ripped it open as I ascended to the eleventh floor. It was a stack of printouts with a note from Edgar. *Trail runs cold after 1990. Could be homeless or dead (unverified).*

I paged through the papers. There was a credit check for Sidney Calkins, a notification of minor emancipation from foster care, and an arrest record. This was the young man who had had a sexual relationship with Johanna Ray.

My phone rang and I answered it without checking ID.

"Hey girly girl, I've been missing you. You have time for a video chat?"

It was Page. We hadn't talked in weeks. Just the sound of her voice was soothing.

"Sure," I said, hitting the camera button. Her kitchen materialized in front of me. Sunny was curled in her dog bed by the door. Page was sitting in the breakfast nook. Her brown hair was tied up behind her.

"I feel like you've dropped off the face of the earth," she said. "It's been ages."

I unloaded everything: what I had discovered about Johanna Ray and Sidney Calkins, Peter's accident, what Veruca had told me about Ian and Esther.

"This is shaping up to be a telenovela," she said after I was finished. "So Ian and Esther got together last summer?"

"Weird, right?"

"I don't know," Page said. "In some ways, it makes sense."

I waited for her to continue.

"I remember that time before you met Peter. You were obsessed with Ian. It's the only stage in our friendship when I have screened your calls. I got so tired of the repetitive loop. He was treating you like shit and you were just going along with it."

"I know, Page. I was there."

"And then that summer you were obsessed with Esther. I never understood why you talked about her so much. But it makes sense. You were picking up on something between them."

"Enlighten me."

"You had this whole narrative going at the time. That Ian could never achieve true intimacy with someone. He had been damaged somehow and you didn't know when. But maybe the reason Esther bothered you was because there was a connection between them."

I had considered this before, of course. But hearing it from someone else made it somehow more real. Yearning for distraction from this conversation, I picked up the stack of documents Edgar had pulled together for me and began sorting through them again.

"And Peter has moved on," Page said. "Are you sure you're OK, Maggie?"

I was focused less on her words and more on an image in front of me. It was below the arrest record for Sid Calkins. It was a grainy mug shot. The clapboard read 11/7/89. Sidney had been arrested and booked into Ithaca County Jail.

"Mags, are you OK?"

"Page, I have to go. I'm sorry." I hit the disconnect button and held the mug shot up into the light. I pushed the dimmer switch up high.

Although he was young in the photo, only about seventeen, Sidney Calkins was clearly and unmistakably a face I recognized.

I got off the phone with Page, hopping a bit with adrenaline. The boy in the photo was the spitting image of Ford. He had the same piercing blue eyes and sandy blond hair. Could he have known Ian's mother? What had that experience done to him? Or was Sidney related to Ford? A cousin? A brother?

I knew I had to be careful proceeding with this. It was potentially explosive. I sent Ford a text saying I would be in Ithaca the next night and wanted to see him. Then I slept fitfully all night waiting to get a reply.

❧

Ford agreed to meet me at a bar called The Queen of Hearts. It was downtown, just off the main commercial strip. I parked on a side street and took a seat with a view of the door. Each booth in the joint was alongside a stained glass window with a different playing card image. I had chosen to sit alongside The Jack of Spades. I couldn't spot a Queen of Hearts anywhere. I ordered a Stoli tonic and nursed it slowly.

After I had drunk half of it, Ford appeared, dressed in faded blue jeans and a matching jacket. I will not deny that watching him walk in was one of the sincerest pleasures of my last few weeks. The guy had undeniable charisma.

"It's great to see you, kid," he said, leaning over and nuzzling me with his stubble.

The bartender knew him and sent him over a Maker's Mark neat. I restrained myself to a single drink. I was driving, after all.

"Wasn't sure I'd see you again after you disappeared the other day," he said. I averted my eyes, flustered.

"I'm actually doing some more research," I said, trying to keep it professional.

"I like the way the research ended last time," he said, a twinkle in his voice. I felt a creeping blush on my cheeks. I hoped the lighting was low enough that he wouldn't see it.

He fixed me with his gaze. I had no idea what he was thinking.

"Did Ian ever tell you that his mother was incarcerated?"

"I hardly knew the guy," Ford said, his congenial smile fading. "We went to a football game once. That's the extent of it."

"I just can't help but wonder if maybe someone connected to that may have had a vendetta against him. The victim's brother, for example. Because the thing is, I have done a little digging and I discovered that Johanna Ray is incarcerated near Tompkins County. Her victim was from Ithaca."

I reached into my handbag. I pulled out the mug shot of Sidney Calkins, taken in 1989. He was a foster child who had been busted for dealing drugs at Cornell. He was also the minor who was assaulted by Johanna Ray.

Ford took the paper from me, gave it a cursory glance, and handed it back.

"Can I tell you something, Maggie? A lot of people on the show didn't like you. They thought you were a bitch. I never thought that. But I'm starting to understand what they might have seen that I didn't. You sleep with me and disappear and now you're here making these ugly accusations. What would you call a guy who did this?"

"Don't you want justice for Ian? He may have been murdered."

"You know one reason people didn't like you, Maggie? It was because you had such a blind spot when it came to Ian. The guy was a first-class asshole. And you're still making excuses for him. If you solve this murder, you will be a hero to no one."

His words stung but I continued."Do you know anyone who might have wanted to hurt Ian?"

He looked at me coldly. "I don't."

He then pulled his wallet out of his back pocket, dropped a twenty on the table, and walked out of the bar.

CHAPTER TWENTY-EIGHT
NOW

I WAS SHAKEN by my encounter with Ford. I felt weak as I walked outside and back to my car. I sat behind the wheel, breathing deeply, my hands shaking.

Why is it that honest criticism hurts so much? I had no doubt that Ford was being entirely candid in what he said to me. Some people we worked with didn't like me. It wasn't a surprise - I had found in life that no criticism ever was - and yet having it confirmed from someone else left me a little off-balance. I had alienated people. And now Ford, a man I liked, thought I was a bitch for digging into the past.

It was amazing, really, how much your own personality is out of your control. I saw this when Riley was growing up. No matter how much I steered or corrected him, his core traits stayed with him. I think this was true of me, too, although my characteristics may not have been innate. I was my mother's child, the accident from college, stuck at the end of my grandparents' long table at holidays, wedged in like someone who just barely fit. I was shaped by the awareness that my mother's life might have been entirely different if I hadn't been born.

For so many years, I felt like the only one burdened with this stamp. Peter was the apple of his mother's eye, Page was a spoiled only child, and my co-stars seemed to have an unshakable confidence that I lacked. I'm sure this is why I was drawn to Ian. He was damaged in a similar way, and yet he was much better at protecting himself. I could recall every sling and arrow – those moments when I didn't feel whole, or when it hurt to hear about other people's good fortune – but he carried on.

I pulled out my phone and typed a text to Detective Shimada. As I sat in my car, twilight was casting shadows around the street. A group of students walked by, chatting back and forth. A barista pulled in a sandwich board and flipped the sign in her front window to *closed.* A man with shaggy hair and a peacoat walked by with a pit bull on a leash.

When my phone buzzed, I answered it without reading the screen.

"Maggie, it's Lou Shimada."

"You got my text?"

"I did, but I'm actually calling you about a different matter. We have begun to narrow in on a possible person of interest in Ian's death. I wonder if you might be able to come into the precinct at your earliest convenience."

This news slapped me out of my present. I had thought she had called so we could talk about Sid's mug shot. They had a person of interest? My mind couldn't quite take it in.

I explained my whereabouts and the difficulty I might have meeting her.

"I can meet you a little closer to where you are," she said. "There is an all-night diner off exit 100 on the 17 E. Can you head that way right now?"

She explained the route in more detail while I consulted Google maps trying to figure out the route. "I think so. I think it will take two and half hours, though."

"No problem for me," Louise said. "I will wait for you."

I headed out, cranking up the music to keep the pace up.

Just off the highway and exit 100, there was a sign with an old man in rocking chair. As I pulled into the parking lot, in the artificial light of the middle of the night, a waitress in the illuminated diner window filled sugar jars while a few patrons dotted the interior.

It was just after midnight. Detective Shimada sat in a booth, drinking a glass of ice water and scrolling through her phone.

"Sorry if I'm late," I said, sliding into the vinyl booth across from her.

The waitress, with a stack of red curls and two coffee pots, walked over and offered me a cup. I accepted a pour from the caffeinated one.

"You had farther to come," she said, smiling warmly and putting her phone back into a windbreaker pocket. "Miss Grayson, I wanted first to thank you. As I reviewed this case, a few things came up that concerned me. The original detectives didn't go over Mr. Dorrit's phone records. If they had, they would have seen that he had a long text conversation during the week that he died, saying things that were not at all consistent with a suicidal person."

"Who were the texts with?" I asked.

"A young woman named Marley Harris," she said.

"Ty's daughter?" I asked.

"Yes, they had been in regular contact between July and August. It was clear that they were having a romance and that her parents were furious about it when they found out."

"I began my own research and discovered this." She reached down to the seat and pulled a photograph out of a manila envelope. She slid the photo across the table.

It was a printout with an image of the interior of a convenience store. There were aisles and cold cases and a man buying something at the register. He had a baseball cap on but there was no mistaking him: it was Ty.

"That's from a gas station in Sea Cliff," Detective Shimada remarked. "Do you recognize that man?"

It really was a stupid question. Ty had a recognizable face.

"I don't believe he would do this."

"He lives on the Upper West Side of Manhattan. Can you think of any reason that he would have been in Sea Cliff in August?"

There was a timestamp in the upper right hand side. It read 8/14/16, the week that Ian died.

"I've only recently reconnected with him. I don't know his habits."

"Do you remember when you reconnected with him?"

"It was at Ian's memorial," I said. "I can't remember the exact date." It would be easy enough to pin down, though. I had kept the program.

"But prior to that, you and Ty were not in close contact?"

"No," I said. "I hadn't seen him in several years. But he mentioned at the memorial that he was just back from London."

"How recently?"

It occurred to me that Ford would know Ty's schedule better than anyone. He had been staying with him around that time. After our encounter tonight, I wasn't sure I should involve him.

"We have done another sweep of Mr. Dorrit's home and discovered some foreign DNA. We asked Mr. Harris to submit a sample and he agreed. It came back as a positive match. Can you think of any reason why Ty Harris's DNA would be found at Mr. Dorrit's residence?"

This was not looking good for him. And, yet, I somehow couldn't believe it. Ty had an affable personality. He seemed forgiving of his ex-wife's decision to move their son away from him and he was friendly enough about Jasmine that I had never detected their history. How could someone with a measured temperament snap like this?

"As I said, I hadn't been in regular contact with Ty or Ian for the last five years. A mutual friend mentioned that they had all gone to a football game at one point. Maybe they were friends."

"Have you ever met Marley?"

"When she was a child, she was on set from time to time. I haven't seen her much in her teenage years."

"And Sara Wilcox, Ty's ex wife? What was your impression of her?"

I told Lou what I remembered. Sara was an energetic strawberry blonde from the Midwest. My impression of her was positive.

"Is she a suspect in this?"

"I'm just trying to eliminate her as a person of interest."

I thought of what Ford had told me, about Ty and Jasmine having an affair in the early days of the show. Marley was about a year older than Riley. She would have been quite young when it ended. Could she have known about her father's affair? Perhaps her mother had told her about it. This might have driven her to seek revenge on her parents by sleeping with Ian.

"Ms. Grayson, when you came to see me the first time, you told me that there might be other people who had motive to kill Ian. I'd just like to go over that information with you again."

She pulled out another printout, this one a screenshot of the journal page I had shown her.

"How did you get involved with Sebastian?" she asked.

I told her the full story: about the business card with the infinity circle, about the parties, about Catharine Nash. I barely paused for breath, finding myself parched by the end. I signaled to the waitress to refill my ice water.

Lou was taking notes in her phone. When she finished, she asked, "Anyone else?"

"Did you get my text about Sidney Calkins?" I asked.

"I did," she said. "I'm not really sure what you're driving at."

"I think I have basically confirmed that my former co-star Ford Sather is related to him. They look enough alike that it's hard to dismiss the coincidence. He told me that his uncle raised him after his mom died. I think he had a younger brother who went to foster care. I think Ford's younger brother wound up the victim of Johanna Ray."

"You said after their mother died, an uncle took him in. Why wouldn't he have taken both boys in?"

"I think they were half brothers. Different fathers. Ford was raised by his father's brother."

"Were you able to confirm this?"

I thought of Ford's angry reaction when I showed him the mug shot. He hadn't denied anything.

"Not yet, but he wasn't pleased when I showed the mug shot to him."

"Why would Ford seek revenge on Ian, though? He was the son of his brother's predator. She's still alive. He could have gone after her."

"Maybe he knew something that we don't." Was it possible that Ford was covering for his younger brother? He might have sought revenge on his rapist by killing her son.

"Miss Grayson, I've been a cop for a long time. And before that I was in the military. We have to go where the evidence leads us. For the time being, we need to settle this matter with Ty Harris. His DNA puts him there, and with these texts between Marley and Ian, it does show possible motive."

The waitress with the big hair and coffee pots stopped by once more. We declined and settled up the bill.

As we parted outside to head back our respective homes, the sun was beginning to crown in the eastern sky.

CHAPTER TWENTY-NINE

NOW

WHEN THE SKYLINE came into view, I was hit with a strange mix of exhaustion and adrenaline. The coffee I had had at the diner was wearing off and with it a feeling of disbelief at all I had experienced in the last twenty-four hours.

Try as I might, I couldn't believe that Ty had killed Ian. And, yet, it was hard to argue with DNA. Was there any way to explain it? I wasn't sure that Ty had ever stepped foot in the cottage. Ian was not one to host parties that I knew of.

As I pulled into a cavernous parking garage near my building, an idea began to percolate. I took a shower, giving myself some time to think, and then pulled on a comfortable pair of yoga pants and a fleece. It was getting colder in the city, the time of the season where you had to layer.

I walked to the 86th Street subway and took a train downtown. The train was nearly empty save for a girl Riley's age feeding a hungry toddler and a man sleeping near a discarded copy of the *Post.*

Years ago my professor at Barnard had given us homework to ride the subway and observe behavior and make up backstories for the strangers I saw. I imagined that the man lived in the Bronx with his mother. He had been laid off from his job selling cars during the recession and was too depressed to find more work. He and his mother loved to eat their dinners on TV trays while watching marathons of *Seinfeld.* I imagined that the chubby toddler was named Clayton. He had been a surprise, a result of a night of clubbing. One day he would tell this story as he ran for political office, running on a family values platform. He would use his own missing dad story to stir sympathy and outrage.

When the subway pulled into Grand Central, I walked to a platform and waited for the uptown train. The 1 would take me to the Upper West Side, and beyond that to Columbia and Morningside Heights. This route was familiar to me in reverse, having gone downtown from campus on days when I had theater tickets or felt the need for a break, but this northern direction felt new, daring. The car was crowded, even at lunchtime, so I gripped a pole, watching two women in chadors chat with a stroller between them, and men and women in business suits scrolling through content on their phones. A group of teenagers got on and, blaring music from a boom box, did an acrobatic dance routine.

"You're going to be a star," a man told them after the routine was over, putting a five-dollar bill into their collection box. I couldn't tell if he was being sincere or not.

The crowd thinned as we got closer to the Columbia stop. When the wheels screeched to a halt and I moved up the steps to the sidewalk above, I felt a flurry of emotions. I had spent so much time here as an undergrad to the point that it was more intimate than the Upper East Side was to me after twenty years. I walked up Broadway until I reached the gates of Barnard and wandered through the campus. It was much as I remembered it.

I thought of myself during those years. I was intimidated by so many of my classmates with their prep school educations and urbane sophistication. We were told to speak from the "I" perspective, not to generalize about others but to own our own thought foundations. When the professors asked for opinions, my classmates always had them. I flailed around, a woman without a perspective, nothing fresh to say.

Where might my life have gone if I had been more like them? It sometimes took me days to open the alumnae quarterly when it showed up in my stack of mail. My classmates were now diplomats, members of Congress, producers of *The Rachel Maddow Show*. I had never been to an alumnae event or been asked to speak at commencement. In the eyes of the Barnard faculty, I was nothing. And in that sense, the needle of my life hadn't moved in twenty-five years.

Across the quad, I heard Corey call my name. He was dressed in a striped sweater and a knit cap, looking like he had just stepped out of a J. Crew catalog. I waved and we met, hugging like old friends.

"I know a few lunch places in this area," he said. "But I know it's your old stomping ground so if you have a preference just holler."

We walked together off campus and through a bustling neighborhood with a Korean BBQ restaurant, an Ethiopian restaurant, and a pool hall.

"That place over there has surprisingly good food," Corey said, gesturing with a mittened hand. We crossed with the light. The bar was half-empty at midday with mahogany booths on one side and a mirrored bar on the other. There was a blackboard with a few food options.

"Have a seat," Corey said, "I'll get our order."

I asked for a cup of chili and some coffee. Corey talked to the bartender until our order was up, returning with Matzo soup for him and ice water for both of us. I ripped open a packet of saltines and broke them over my mound of beans.

"So I've got something cooking," Corey said, slicing off a bit of Matzo ball with his spoon. "My friend and I are writing a musical that is a queer tribute to *Buffy the Vampire Slayer*. I'm going to be playing Xander."

I swallowed some chili and congratulated him. He would be good for that role. It was just as well that I couldn't sing or dance or I might be jealous.

"We're going to rent a stage in the New Year. Hope to see you there," he said.

"Wouldn't miss it," I said. "I wanted to ask you something. It's a little awkward."

"Shoot," he said.

"When you were staying with me, a box arrived from Jasmine. Do you remember that?"

"Sure," he said, taking another bite of Matzo.

"There was a zip drive in it that fell out when I brought the box up from my lobby. I looked at it."

Corey took a sip of water. His face was pale. He waited for me to continue.

"I'm sorry. I know that was an invasion. I feel bad. But I saw something on it and I wanted to ask you about it."

He sat back in the booth, crossing his arms across his chest. His soup sat half-eaten in front on him.

"The porn video that Ian was in. Why did you have it?"

"You think you have a right to ask me about content on my private zip drive," he said. It was a statement, not a question.

"Corey, I don't blame you for being mad at me. But you have to understand that I'm trying to get to the bottom of this. They may arrest Ty, you know."

"Why would they arrest him?"

"Ian was sleeping with Ty's daughter Marley. They found his DNA in Ian's cottage."

"You know this, how?"

"I've been talking to a detective. I'm the reason she opened this case," I said. My words felt like sand.

"Jesus, Maggie. I'm trying to hold it together here, even though you have just broadly implied that I might be involved in the murder of a homophobic asshole."

"I believe you, Corey, I just want to know why you had that video."

"I found it, Maggie. I was housesitting for Jasmine a while back and it was on her drive. How did she get it? I don't know. Maybe someone sent it to her. A friend watched it and recognized her ex-husband."

"I'm sorry," I said. I felt horrible.

"You know, Maggie, I have put up with a lot of shit in my life. I expected more from you. I thought we were friends. Isn't that why you let me stay with you?"

I knew not to say anything. I didn't look up until I knew he was gone.

CHAPTER THIRTY
THEN

As soon as she was done with school for the day, Christiana would grab a book from the library and walk up the hill. Taking a seat beneath a tree, turning pages until the sunlight dipped below the hill, she felt transported to other realms, compelled by heroines facing hardships far more dramatic than her own. There were so many good books. She loved starting and finishing one every day. When she closed the book a few hours later, she had completed a journey unlike the one the previous day.

When she was done reading, she would climb a tree, way up to the highest branch, and view the world from below. Everything seemed small when she was up in those branches. She would lie there, hearing her mother call her name when dinner was ready, and relish the idea that she was someplace no one could find her. She loved it when her mother boiled over, trudging up the hill to drag her home. She would watch her mother pace around below, confused, frustrated. Her mother never figured out that Christiana was above her.

Sometimes the acolytes would come, singing together as they picked fruit for an evening pie. Other times it was Tamberlain who appeared, pulling out her pouch of tobacco and carefully rolling a cigarette in thin paper.

She and her mother had been at Concordia for a few months. They had moved into one of the A frames, between Tamberlain and her sons on one side and Johanna on the other. Johanna's son had come to visit, too, just for a few weeks. He was a few years older and liked to join her in the apple orchard. He taught her to climb a tree. Then abruptly, without a goodbye, he was gone. Johanna had not mentioned him again.

One day, when she was high up in the treetops, she saw Johanna and Sid. It was inevitable that she would bring him here. It was the most private place on the land. They stood together, lost in each other, and she could hear their soft murmurs. Sid moved down her neck, kissing it, and then rested his lips on her breast, biting it. Johanna pushed back her head and moaned so loudly that he looked around nervously, afraid of prying eyes.

Johanna bent down, unzipping his jeans, and now she was on her knees in front of him, bobbing her head over his erect cock. He threw his head back, moaning.

Farther away was the patch of land with the houses, and beyond that the school, the chapel, and the fields. In the distance, there was a flashing light. First she couldn't make out whether it was red or yellow, but as it grew she saw that it was not one but many lights, a stream of them like a moving river. They were pulsing over the hills and onto the land. Cars were stopping and there were figures, so small they were like mice, walking in two-by-two. Noise grew too, and an acolyte ran up the hill towards Johanna and Sid, calling out to them. They parted, but not before she saw them. They sloped down the hill, following her lead, unsure.

Christiana climbed down the tree trunk as fast as she could, ripping her shirt on a branch as she fell to the soft earth. She landed on her feet like a cat and ran down the hill. There were men and women in blue Mylar coats, moving in and out of the chapel and the school. When they turned their backs, yellow letters spelled out *FBI* on their jackets.

In the distance, on the hill, Johanna and Tamberlain stood together. She waved to them. They didn't wave back.

She found Sid outside the school. "Fuck, they arrested Johanna and Tamberlain, " he said. "Someone turned them in."

She stepped back, not understanding his words, and ran back to the place from which she had come. Johanna and Tamberlain were still there. She saw now that their arms were tied behind their backs. Johanna was looking directly at her, trying to reassure her that everything would be okay. She had never done this before.

Two men in blue coats appeared and stood on either side of Johanna and Tamberlain, guiding them down the incline to a parked squad car.

She walked up to it. The window was cracked open. "It's OK, Christiana, you can stay here tonight," Johanna said. "Find your mom. Don't worry. She will take care of you."

Christiana stepped back as the cruiser turned its engine and pulled away. She began choking on her sobs, standing frozen on the level earth. After a while, she felt a strong set of arms around her. She turned to see her mother's lithe body and auburn curls framed by the fading blue sky. She yearned for her mother's comfort, but at this moment her embrace felt static, cold. In the sky above, the moon had begun to appear, a faint milky light.

❧

After the FBI raid at Concordia, Sid began sleeping in the bus depot. The last ride, from Buffalo, pulled it at 1:30 and after that he could curl up in a sleeping bag near the vending machines and get a few hours. When it got busy again at 7, he made his way downtown. He had befriended a clerk at the Mother Hen convenience store who gave him free coffee and breakfast. After that, he rode his skateboard across town to the Cornell campus.

After a few months, he had a steady clientele. He stopped in a few dorms and houses, in dining services, and then made his way back downtown. He could usually clear $100 a day, enough that he might be able to find housing, but he needed to save everything he was making. He didn't plan to stay in Ithaca much longer.

The FBI raid had resulted in two fast-track trials. He had to make an appearance at both, answering the lawyers' invasive questions, and standing by as Johanna and Tamberlain were both sentenced. He wasn't allowed to talk to either of them but occasionally Tamberlain's son, Rustin, would find him at the Mother Hen and convey a message. The land had been seized and would be put up at auction, but Tamberlain was defiant that their community would continue in some form.

Sid could tell Rustin was lying when he talked about Johanna. Whatever she was telling him would be too painful for Sid to take in. His friend was protecting him.

Sid continued on for a few months in Ithaca, storing his profits in a locker at the bus depot, and eventually gaining legal emancipation from foster care. He was caught by police once, selling to a narc on campus, but they let him off easy.

One day Rustin stopped by the Mother Hen, asking after his friend. The clerk said he hadn't seen Sid recently. When he went to the depot, the woman working there told him that Sid had boarded a bus to New York City. None of them ever heard from him again.

CHAPTER THIRTY-ONE

NOW

After my encounters with Ford and Corey, I found myself unwilling to make an effort with my daily routine. I stopped going to yoga and spent half the night zoned out in front of the TV. When Ian died, I was so fixated on the circumstances that I didn't realize how my investigation might hurt others. Now that I was beginning to understand its reach, I was reluctant to be involved. I would leave this to the professionals.

Peter had broken his leg and was holed up in his executive suite in Midtown. I hadn't talked to him since the text exchange about Sebastian Detlefsen. The day would come when there would be a knock on my door and I would be served with divorce papers. I was ready for it. My marriage was over, my son was beginning a new phase of life without me, and I was on my own for the first time in a long time.

The days began to blend together, and move along more quickly than I might have imagined given how little I was actually accomplishing. My life began to feel like summers when I was growing up, the endless tedium that could make even the most indifferent student long for a Back To School sale.

One day, as I was watering plants in my living room while rocking out to the *Cruel Intentions* soundtrack, my cell phone rang.

"Maggie, hi. It's Ty."

I hadn't talked to him since that dinner at my mother's.

I wasn't sure how to greet him so I started babbling about my empty nest. When I paused for breath, I asked him how he was.

"The police think I had something to do with Ian's death."

I feigned surprise, letting him fill me in on the details I already knew from my meeting with Detective Shimada.

"Maggie, I'm calling you because I trust you. You have always been there for me in the past." This was typical of Ty: he had a hyperbolic way of talking to and about people including some he hardly knew. That hadn't changed.

"I don't believe you did this, Ty. I can imagine how devastated you were when you learned about Ian and Marley, but I don't believe you are capable of this."

When he spoke next, he was choked up. "It's not looking good," he said. "My ex-wife runs a nursery in Chicago and they think they can prove that the digitalis plant originated through an invoice at her company. Will a jury believe that?"

"Why were you in Sea Cliff?" I asked, not sure I wanted the answer.

Ty sighed and paused. "I trust you so I will tell you. I'm not proud of this. When I found out that Ian was sleeping with Marley, I confronted him about it. First he denied it, but when I showed him Marley's phone he was caught. He was a real prick about it. He said that Marley was a legal adult and could make her own choices."

I waited for him to continue.

"I got seriously worked up. With Sara taking Asher back to Chicago and now this, I just felt so out of control of my life. So one night in mid August I went to Ian's cottage. He wasn't home but I got in through an unlocked sliding door. I had a gun, Maggie. I was going to kill him. But when I heard him approaching with a woman, I hid in the hallway closet. I could see them through the slatted door. He was cutting lines, snorting coke with her, feeling her up."

"That must have been hard to witness."

"But it wasn't Marley. I felt such relief. He was with some other woman. I lost the will to kill him. And when they went to the bedroom, I left the same way I came in."

"Did you tell the police this?"

"How could I? I seem guilty as sin."

"That woman is a potential suspect, Ty. She might have killed him."

"I know. But I'm not naïve, Maggie. Innocent people have gone to prison on far less evidence than this."

"What did the woman look like?"

"It was dark in the hallway, but she was white and blonde. Older than Marley definitely."

So it might have been Esther. Maybe what Veruca told me was true. Ian was sleeping with Esther and Marley around the same time. Perhaps Esther figured it out.

"I'm so sorry you are going through this, Ty. Is there anything I can do to help?"

"Marley is not speaking to me right now. She hasn't answered a call or text since the word got out that the police think I did it. I'm wondering if you could have your mother check in on her. I just want to know that she's alright."

"No problem," I said. Despite her own occasional parental indifference, my mother was good in a crisis. I had full faith that she would drop in on Marley and make things better.

"I might have something that could help you," I said, getting up from my seat on the sofa and walking over to my dining room table. "You've known Ford for a while, right?"

"Yeah, since grad school. We both were in the Drama program at Yale."

"Did you know his uncle, who raised him?"

"Sure. His name was Jason Sather. He was my professor at one point."

"And Ford was an only child?"

"Gosh, I don't remember. Ford still talks a lot about his uncle but not a lot about his life before he lived with him."

So if, as I suspected, Sidney Calkins was Ford's half-brother, he somehow ended up in foster care after their mother died.

"I'm going to send you a scan of a police report for a young man named Sidney Calkins. I think he might be Ford's half-brother. If you can confirm that, your defense lawyer can raise doubt. What happened to this guy? He was traumatized as a teenager and may have sought revenge on his predator's son. Doubt is all it takes in cases like this."

"Thanks, Maggie. Send it to me and I'll give it to my lawyer."

"Can I ask you something, Ty?"

"Sure."

"Your affair with Jasmine, when did it start?"

Ty exhaled. "You know, back in college when I met Sara I thought I was the luckiest man in the world. But after Marley was born, she changed. She resented the fact that I was at the set all day and that she was home caring for a newborn. If we had never left the Midwest, we could have lived near her mother and sisters. It all would have been so much easier for her."

I winced a bit at this revelation. It reminded me of things Peter had said to me over the years. Men can be so selfish when babies are born, taking their wives' exhaustion as a personal rejection. If they only knew what was really going on.

"And Jasmine was so understanding. Her marriage to Ian wasn't going well and her mother had just died. She was empathetic in a way Sara never was."

"When was this?"

"Marley was born in 1997, so I'm guessing the affair started in 1998."

Ty kept talking, about his attempt after the affair to reconcile with Sara, about the surprise of her second pregnancy with Asher, about the end with Jasmine just as she and Ian were divorcing.

I was only half-listening. Instead I was thinking back to the party I did with Jasmine. She told me her mother died when she was just out of a high school.

"Ty, I'm sorry to cut you off, but do you remember how Mrs. Dakari died?"

"Breast cancer," he said. "And Dakari is a stage name. Jasmine's mother's last name was Longo."

I hung up with Ty, feeling a new surge of adrenaline. I was done with the case for good, I told myself, and I meant it. But I just had one more thing I needed to do first.

CHAPTER THIRTY-TWO
NOW

THE FESTIVAL WAS in a church parking lot in a neighborhood in Brooklyn I had never seen before. Vendors were setting up food booths when I arrived, Frank Sinatra music piped in through hanging speakers. I wandered around for a bit, buying myself a pastry and coffee, and made my way to the Longo Foods Booth. There were two young men standing behind it. The table was piled high with Mylar bags full of black candy. There were braided breads, stacks of herbs, cans of olive oil.

"You found us," a voice said behind me. I turned to see Jasmine, dressed in a beanie, yoga pants, and a red puffy jacket approaching with a steaming cup of coffee. She gestured behind her. "Anthony, Matty I would like to introduce you to Maggie Grayson. Maggie, these are my two favorite cousins." They smiled warmly, their breath visible in the cold.

One of them extended a sample platter to me with small pieces of candy. "Would you like to try our signature product?" I took a large piece and put it on my tongue. It tasted like burnt sugar.

"Our charcoal candy is a big hit each year," Jasmine said, ducking underneath the booth and emerging on the other side nearer to her cousins. "We sell about a hundred pounds of it in two days."

In front of me on the booth table, there was a heaping stack of dolls. Le Befana was a little old lady in an apron with a straw broom. On her back was a black satchel with charcoal candy tucked inside. This was an Italian tradition for the Epiphany. Riley was a little old for this, but I thought it might be fun to introduce a new tradition this year over the holidays. I took three dolls and handed over a fifty-dollar bill. Matty made change for me.

Jasmine rooted around some boxes in back. "Boys, I'm going to take a break to talk to Maggie. You can text me if things get crazy." She emerged again from underneath the booth and walked me through the parking lot. "I know a place just across the way. It's warm."

"Your family is well represented today. I thought you grew up in Malibu Canyon."

"I did. But my mother's family has owned a grocery store in Brooklyn for over a hundred years."

"So you're Italian," I said.

"With a name like Dakari, you might not think so. There was already a Jasmine Longo in SAG. Dakari is my middle name."

"Right."

She had walked us away from the parking lot, across the street to a restaurant. Inside, there were small round tables with blue and white tablecloths. Two old men sat at a table playing chess. The menu was written in colored chalk on a blackboard hanging above the cash register.

"They have great Panini here," she said, taking a seat facing the door. "And good desserts."

A waitress took our orders and we made small talk until the food arrived. When I bit into my basil and mozzarella sandwich, it was so good I nearly moaned. I took a swig of lemon soda. It was crisp and cold.

"This is delicious," I said. I hadn't had any real food in days.

"Right?" She said. "Always take food recommendation from a native." She bit into her sandwich and chewed for a moment. "So what did you want to talk to me about?"

"I've been doing a bit of research. I think Ian may not have killed himself."

"Right, you've mentioned that," she replied.

"Do you ever remember Ian talking about a place called Concordia?"

"A commune near Ithaca?"

"Right," I said. "It was owned by a woman named Tamberlain Wallace.

She had a vision of creating a society without men. She bought land in upstate New York and a group of women moved there with their children. They created a school with their own curriculum and had religious services where they took communion on a sliced apple."

"A sliced apple?" she said.

"It was meant to take back the false myth of the fall. They believed that the Eve myth was created to subjugate women and establish the patriarchy. They created a liturgy that honored her, including a ceremonial bite of an apple at the end."

"But boys were there?"

"It was a matriarchal society so there were no adult men living there. If the women had underage sons, they were welcome until they turned eighteen." I pulled out the ethnography and opened to a photo of a group of women standing together in front of a two-story school.

I pointed an index finger to a brunette in the back row. She had her hands on the shoulders of a nine-year-old girl. The woman's black hair was flowing in the wind.

"She looks like my mother," Jasmine said.

"I was talking to Ty the other night," I said. "And he told me that your mother died of breast cancer about eighteen years ago. Why did you lie to me about this, Jasmine?"

She was averting her eyes, as if distracted by something on the street.

"My father was a good man," Jasmine said. "For a while, we were happy. But then my mother fell in love with this bastard she met at a spiritual retreat. He was so charming and charismatic that she was swept away. When my father found out, my older sister and I decided to stay with him. My younger sister was only eight and went with mom. By the time my mom finally wised up to what a bastard this guy was, it was too late. He had molested Christiana."

"So after she discovered your stepfather's abuse, your mom ended up moving to Concordia with your sister. What I didn't know until recently was that Ian came to visit that summer, just before the feds shut the place down. He was seventeen at the time. And he and your sister knew each other briefly. Something happened between them."

"He took advantage of her," Jasmine said. "She was already traumatized and he made it worse."

"And you just figured it out last summer, didn't you? When your sister killed herself? She left a note that confessed her long-held secret. Her sister's onetime husband had molested her when they were living at Concordia."

I had found an obituary online for Christiana Longo. She had taken her own life in June. She was thirty-five with a history of substance abuse and homelessness. I wasn't sure that I had all the details right, but after learning what Ian had done with Marley, I realized that he was as much a predator as his mother. In a way, I had been one of the lucky ones. His darkest moments were with others.

"What would you do for your son?" Jasmine asked me. Her eyes were a soft pool of brown, both sad and resigned. "Anything, right? Christiana was like my baby. When my parents split up, and my mom left with her, there was a hole in my heart."

"But somehow you never knew that she and Ian knew each other. He was so private about his mother that you never put it together. And when your sister did, probably after you were cast on a soap opera with him, she said nothing."

"My sister never got the help she needed. I paid for many therapists but she just couldn't look deeply at the abuse or who had done it. Ian and I were together so briefly. I think if we had stayed together longer, she would have told me."

I was less sure of that, but I said nothing. Abusers often know how to manipulate their victims into silent complicity. It was how they kept from getting caught.

"That was clever of you, making me think that Sebastian knew something about your mother's suicide," I said. "Is that why you agreed to do the party? So you could perpetuate the idea that Sebastian was behind this?"

Jasmine lifted a hand and began messaging her neck. The weight of her confession seemed to be hitting her.

"How did you figure this out?" she asked.

"At first I had some wrong information. The local gossip in Ithaca was that the FBI raided Concordia after a boy drowned, but that's not true. It happened after a resident went to the police. Her nine-year-old daughter had been sexually abused by an older boy who was visiting for the summer. The FBI opened a case and found that a minor boy and his mother were both sexual predators. They had enough to put Johanna away, but Ian was given a second chance and sent back to his father in California."

"I didn't know," she said. "I married the guy and I didn't know. My sister had been so terrified by that experience that she never talked about it. It took her until last summer to name him. When I told her that we were back together, she found the strength to tell me."

How horrible this must have been for them. Jasmine, lost in the bliss of an unexpected reunion, and her sister having to unburden this horrible family secret.

"I'm not going to turn you in, Jasmine. I understand what Christiana's suicide must have done to you. I'm sure this has been agonizing for you. But you should know that the police think Ty did it. He went there one night to confront Ian about what he was doing with Marley. The police found Ty's DNA in the house. They have a surveillance video image of Ty in the area."

"I will never let Ty go to prison. You have my word on that. If it gets to that point, I will confess."

In that moment, I believed her.

What I knew now was that Ian was not a good man. I was amazed at my capacity to think otherwise. Ty and Jasmine had both taken the law in their own hands, but I would leave it to the police to sort it out. They had to prove what had happened that week. I wasn't sure they would be able to.

Across the street, the festival had picked up. Hanging lights had been switched on and the music cranked up. Frank Sinatra was singing a Christmas tune. Maybe I would stop back for a few minutes and see what else they were selling. Then I would find the subway and take it home.

EPILOGUE

When I arrived at the park on that crisp December morning, I took a seat on a park bench and removed the top from my Acropolis cup. The coffee was still steaming so I waited to take my first sip. A homeless man in a green Army jacket was eating a tinfoil take out container of rice with peppers. Pigeons pecked at breadcrumbs near a statue. The sun was out, casting rays through milky white clouds.

Catharine Nash appeared a few minutes later, dressed in running gear, her blonde hair tied up in a ponytail. She would fit in well in this neighborhood, mistaken for a nanny or a grad student. She took a seat next to me on the bench.

She had called me a few days before, while I was in Westchester looking at properties with Page. After twenty-five years in the city, I was thinking more seriously about making a change. We had toured a few colonials and a rustic bungalow near her place in Katonah. It was easier to imagine living out of the city now that the auditions were drying up, but my mind wasn't quite made up.

"So I assume your name isn't Catharine Nash," I said.

"Allow me to introduce myself," she said. "My name is Leneve Wilson. I am an FBI agent."

Could have fooled me. This woman was good.

"I am in charge of a task force called The Infinity Circle. We have been surveilling Sebastian Detlefsen for a few years. He came here originally in 1984 to study psychology at Cornell. A few years ago, he approached Julian Barker about licensing some of her characters for a theme park he was designing. His plan was to create an amusement park that featured sets and characters from popular television shows. They wanted an interactive experience, kind of like an adult Disneyland. They would design sets to look like popular TV shows and hire actors to reprise their roles. Fans would be attracted naturally to these experiences."

"How did you get involved?" My coffee was going cold in my hands as I absorbed this news.

"The agency got wind of some communication between Mr. Detlefsen and a foreign government. We are making a case that he intended to use these parks to procure soft data on American test subjects."

"How?"

"The theory was that many Americans feel an attachment to television characters. TV viewers have certain traits in common with cult members. This is how the indoctrination would begin. It would seem pleasurable at first. But then they planned to use the actors to recruit people."

"Recruit them?"

"Sell them on ideas that were foreign to them. Would they be more receptive to a new ideology, for example, if a beloved TV character presented the ideas to them? This is what they aimed to find out. They were going to test this out and sell the results to people who might be able to use it against us. A foreign faction, for instance, might influence voters in a presidential election."

"You said you're building a case?"

"A few years ago, Detlefsen had his first test subject, a man named Sylvester Gatewood. He had worked with Julian many years ago when she was the head writer for *All My Children*. They were friends. But after he didn't advance, Detlefsen had the idea to approach Ian Dorrit. He tried to recruit him and got further. But he backed out, too."

"How did Ian get involved?"

"Sebastian has a porn business to cover his more nefarious activities. He and Mr. Dorrit met at a poker tournament in Vegas last year. He offered to relieve Ian's gambling debts if he starred in one of his productions."

So the video I had seen was real.

"Why do you need me?"

"As I said, we are building a case against Sebastian Detlefsen and we want to get you on board. You and Mr. Gatewood can provide needed testimony."

I was still trying to take all of this in. "What about those parties? The business cards?"

"The cards were from the FBI. I pitched the idea to Sebastian and he liked it. The parties were his idea: they had to first check to see if you were psychologically weak enough for recruit. So they invited you to participate in the plays and then kicked it up a notch by messing with your personal history. If he determined that you were malleable, he was going to offer you big bucks to play your character at the first park. This was all going to be marketed very innocently. He pretended to be a fan of your show."

"How did you get involved?" I asked, not sure if I was pushing too far.

"The FBI set it up. Sebastian believed my cover story and hired me."

"I feel so stupid," I said.

"Don't be too hard on yourself, Ms. Grayson. This was a very sophisticated plan. Sebastian has been studying soft data collection for years. This was carefully orchestrated."

"And Ty? Does he have anything to do with this?"

"As of right now, the two cases are unrelated. I have talked to Detective Shimada and we are continuing to monitor any developments. The police believe that Ty killed Ian because he was sleeping with his daughter. There is no evidence that Ty and Sebastian are working together."

I knew better. Ty had not killed Ian. Jasmine had done it to avenge her sister's abuse. The previous summer, she had contacted Ian and visited him at the cottage, where she slipped the digitalis into one of his Vitamin Waters. Knowing that Ian had a black thumb, she went back one night and planted the digitalis plant in a part of his yard. What she didn't know was that Ty would also show up that week to confront him. He left without harming Ian, but not without leaving behind a few strands of his hair.

I was hoping that as Detective Shimada dug deeper, she would uncover some evidence that Jasmine had been to Sea Cliff that week. Surely there was a surveillance video, a gas station receipt, something that placed her in the area.

I knew that there were those who would judge me for not turning Jasmine in. If the police found out, I could go to jail myself. I was prepared to face the consequences for my decision. Ian had created lasting damage in many people's lives. I simply could not be complicit anymore.

Agent Leneve Wilson and I exchanged a few more words before she stood up and walked away. She left me with her business card, with an embossed seal from the FBI. Her office was in Midtown.

I lingered a bit, watching a gaggle of toddlers walk by, holding onto red rings and following their teacher. The morning sunlight was glinting off the wet pavement as I got up and headed out of the park. I picked up the pace, moving past joggers and families with strollers. As I cleared a copse of trees, there was a mailbox on the corner. I pulled an envelope out of my bag, looked at the address one last time, and dropped it in.

She would get it in a few days. I wasn't sure what she would think of it, or even if she would open it. I wasn't seeking forgiveness or absolution. It simply had to be done. I had written it the previous week on a piece of monogrammed stationary my mother-in-law gave me years ago.

Dear Esther:

During the summer you interned for the show, I did something to you for which I am greatly ashamed. I don't expect you to forgive me but I want you to know that I have not forgotten what I did or the impact it had on you and others. I won't offer excuses except to say that I have seen the error of my ways and I vow to do better. That is all I can offer you. I hope it is better than the alternative, which is to say nothing.

I had signed it with a single initial. I wasn't sure how the note would be received, but I had included my return address if she wanted to say more to me. I didn't expect a response.

As I walked further away from the park, past sunlight-dappled trees and brownstone stoops, the pulse of the city picked up. I moved with it, disappearing into a crowd of strangers.

THE END

www.ingramcontent.com/pod-product-compliance
Lightning Source LLC
LaVergne TN
LVHW041928090826
845145LV00017B/2295

* 9 7 8 1 7 3 5 7 0 3 5 0 3 *